A Slice of Sin

Edited By

Cherry Wild and Sophia Soror

This book first published for Kindle in 2015.

Published in the United States by A Two Dame Production, LLC
Seattle, Washington.
http://www.two-dames.com

First paperback edition.

ISBN: 0-9970011-1-9
ISBN-13: 978-0-9970011-1-2

Cover photography by
Andrew S. Williams
http://www.journeysincolor.net

FEATURING STORIES BY

Michael Bracken
Morrigan Cox
Paul Henry
Rachael Knight
Lynn Lake
Parker Lee
Aiden McKenna
Chase Morgan
Leah Mueller
Sophia Soror
Autmn Tooley
Alegra Verde
Cherry Wild

CONTENTS

FROM THE EDITORS

In 2014, Cherry was writing a literary novel. Then, the sex scenes started taking on lives of their own, becoming far longer and far more detailed than any literary novel could rightly justify. This was not the first time this had happened while Cherry was working on a novel. She admitted to Sophia how much fun she was having writing these scenes. Then, Sophia admitted that she, too, had a collection of smutty stories that she had written.

After various chats over drinks, a deal was struck. "A year from now, we are going to publish a collection of erotic stories." While the original idea was just for stories written by the two of us, the idea soon evolved. Once we came out of the erotica-writing closet, we discovered that nearly every writer we talked to had a little erotica tucked away, like a scandalous and private secret. This inspired us to dream bigger and start a publishing house, instead of just publishing a one-off collection. In short order, we built a website, formed an LLC, and A Two Dame Production emerged, suggestively licking her lips at the world.

Compiling this collection has been a wonderful ride and we are excited to share these stories with you. There is a broad selection of stories, which are sure to keep you coming back for second and third helpings. So now, dear readers, a year after making that promise to each other, we are thrilled to present *A Slice of Sin*, the first in a series of anthologies celebrating one of the most primal human forces: sexual desire. We know you will have as much pleasure reading it as we did compiling it.

Enjoy!

xx
Cherry and Sophia

THE STAND IN
Chase Morgan

"How about that one?"

"Shhh, someone's going to hear you."

"No one's going to hear, the music's too loud and they're all involved in their own conversations." John looked at Kelly with anticipation. "So?"

Kelly knew he was right. The couple next to her had been head-to-head whispering and giggling for the last hour and the guy sitting next to John was glued to the game on the big screen. She loved this bar—it wasn't too loud and there was always a good mix of people, the perfect place to play their game.

"It feels wrong."

"Babe, this is our game, and no one in here knows they're a part of it. This is just fantasy, your fantasy, so how about it?"

"Well then…no. He doesn't quite do it for me." Kelly did like this game, but she always had to get over the mental obstacle of objectifying strangers. A mischievous smile grew on her face as she scanned the bar. The guy talking to a girl on the other side of the room was cute, but not fantasy good. No, for this game she could have whomever she wanted. "That one," she said, with a discreet nod.

John tried to follow her eyes without being obvious. "Which one? I see two."

"That one—black shirt and jeans, they just walked in about 15 minutes ago." Kelly smiled at her husband. She loved their secret little games. They started years ago whispering dirty things while out to dinner. The point was to tease the other into making the first move. Their game evolved into subtle groping, discreet flashing when she was sans panties,

1

and sending risqué pictures from the restroom while the other was still at the table with friends.

On game nights, the sex usually started in the car before they even left the parking lot. But the game took a turn last month while they were watching a video in bed together. Kelly let it slip that she wished she were the girl on the screen, getting fucked and having a cock in her mouth.

"Is that something you'd like to do?" John asked as he fucked her from behind.

"Yeah, I think so," she said with a little trepidation.

John increased his pace; "I would love to watch you get fucked while you suck my cock."

That night marked the next step in their torrid little game. On their next date, John pointed to a guy and asked her if he was suitable, then another, and another. By the end of the night he was asking her to point the guys out, just as he was doing tonight.

She enjoyed the thought of another man, and that her husband was so accepting of her depraved fantasy. Kelly didn't know if she would ever follow through with it, but the thought was exciting.

"Why that one?"

"I like his shoulders and arms," Kelly smiled, "and I'll bet he's got nice legs too."

"He looks like a soccer player or something like that," John added, "One of those young athletic guys that can probably go all night long."

Her pussy moistened as her mind began to drift. She imagined him taking his shirt off, revealing broad shoulders. She wondered if he was wearing underwear or went commando like John.

"Do you think he's hung?" John asked

Kelly's nipples hardened. "Shhh, not too loud," but his question was perfectly timed; she was imagining looking down past the man's waist to see a bulge in his jeans. Sometimes she thought John could actually read her mind.

"Babe, no one can hear us. So what do you think?"

"He's young and fit. —Yes, I think he's got a nice cock." She felt John's hand sliding up her leg. Butterflies ran through her stomach, she wanted him to slip a finger inside her. Kelly parted her legs, but they were too exposed on the barstool and he stopped mid-thigh. "I'm not wearing panties and if you keep that up I'm going to slide off this bar stool."

"We should pick him up and take him with us," John teased. "Every guy that age has a MILF fantasy."

Kelly felt John drawing lazy circles on her thigh, the same circles he liked to draw around her clit. Her imagination kept pace with John's words. She imagined kissing the stranger, running her hands down his muscled torso, and unzipping his pants for the first peek at what was inside. The excitement of seeing a stranger's cock made her body shiver with good anxiety.

"Maybe we could stop at that abandoned lot on the way home and bend you over the car."

There was no question that John was winning the game tonight. Kelly's pussy was slick with need, making her squirm in her seat.

John leaned over and whispered in her ear, "You probably couldn't wait that long, you'd be in the back seat kissing him before we left the parking lot. Knowing that I'm watching in the mirror, you'd throw me a wink just before pulling his cock out and wrapping your lips around it. Would you like to suck his cock while I watch you in the mirror? Would it turn you on to know that I was sitting right in front of you, hard as a rock, desperately looking for a place to pull over so we could fuck you?"

"OK. You win, I'm soaking wet, let's get out of here." Kelly quickly finished her drink and grabbed John's hand as she headed for the door. At this point, she couldn't be trusted to keep her fingers out of her skirt.

"I thought you felt bad fantasizing about strangers," John chuckled in the parking lot. He opened the car door and stole a quick kiss before she sat down.

Kelly buried a finger inside her swollen pussy before John had time to close the door. Her imagination took her past the scene John built in the bar. Now she was in a place where the man could take her from behind and John's cock could fill her mouth.

"Are you thinking about him, sliding his cock inside you?"

Kelly couldn't speak; she simply reached over and unzipped his pants as soon as he shut the door. She was lost in fantasy during their drive. She subconsciously stroked John's cock while working two fingers in her slick pussy. Her mind jumped with John's words.

"Do you think he would eat your pussy before he fucked it?"

John's words transformed her fingers into the stranger's tongue.

"Maybe he would drive his tongue inside your wet pussy...after he fucked it."

John knew that was one of her favorite things and she loved him for it.

"We haven't even talked about what will happen when he and I are ready to come," John whispered, "Can you imagine two guys coming at the same time?"

Kelly imagined two cocks erupting and was about to explode with her own orgasm when she felt the car stop.

Momentarily thrown off she opened her eyes to see that John had pulled into the abandoned lot he mentioned earlier.

"I've got a surprise for you," John said.

"What is it?" Kelly begged, "I'm about to explode."

"You'll see...when I'm ready to show you."

There was no question he'd won the game tonight; in fact this was one for the record books. He'd taken the teasing to a new level and she was so close to orgasm, the wind could set her off.

"You win honey, I've got to come, please, let me come."

John leaned over and kissed her, placing his hand over hers while she rubbed her pussy. "I want you to suck my cock." After another quick kiss he opened his door and stepped outside.

By the time he walked around and opened Kelly's door, his pants were unbuttoned and his thick rod stood out. Kelly reached for it, but John grabbed her hand and pulled her out of the seat. "Stand up and suck my cock," he ordered.

Kelly did as she was told. She stood from her seat and bent at the waist, taking John's cock in her mouth. His flesh felt good against her tongue. She felt the ridges on his shaft and tasted the pre-come as she engulfed him.

"What're you thinking about?" John asked. "Are you thinking about sucking my cock while that stranger flips your skirt up and gets his first look at your beautiful pussy?"

The depraved thought filled her mind. She knew this wasn't socially acceptable behavior; what would her friend Tami think if she knew Kelly wanted to get fucked by some stranger while she sucked her husband's cock? But then again, it felt so right, so fun, and so naughty.

Kelly moaned as she sucked her husband's cock and let her fingers find her pussy again. A cool breeze passed over her wet lips, increasing the sensation and sending a shiver down her spine.

"He's kneeling down behind you, holding your ass in both hands and running his tongue the full length of your pussy."

Kelly was about to explode. She found her clit, imagining it was the stranger's tongue, and within seconds felt the orgasm running its course. She shuddered as the electricity coursed through her body. A deep moan escaped her lips, still stretched around her husband's cock.

"Did that feel good?"

"Mmm hmmm." Kelly continued sucking his cock.

"Turn around, I want to taste you."

Kelly did as she was told. She turned and leaned forward on the car, presenting her throbbing pussy to John.

"Can you see him in front of you with his thick cock in hand? He's waiting for you to take it in your mouth." She felt him lift her skirt and realized that they were both still clothed for the most part.

"Would you like to suck his cock while I eat your pussy?"

Kelly shuddered when his tongue slid past her swollen lips and deep into her honey pot.

"Eat my pussy baby," she moaned. "Eat my pussy before he fucks it."

John was an incredible lover, and for almost two decades he continued to surprise her. She was always quick to recover from an orgasm and knew that he could bring her to another very quickly. His warm tongue slithered between her wet lips, but she needed more, she wanted to be filled by a cock. "I want you to fuck me baby."

Kelly felt John's tongue, and then, if she didn't know any better, would swear that she felt the head of his cock parting her lips too. Now she was certain, that was the head of a cock spreading her lips and working deeper inside, but John was still on his knees behind her. "What's that? Oh God it feels so good." Kelly pulled her skirt up to see John gently working a large dildo into her pussy.

"Told you I had a surprise." John wore the biggest grin she had ever seen.

The dildo was buried inside her now. She was amazed how real it felt. The head was bulbous and she felt the ridges on the shaft as he worked it in and out of her pussy.

Her juices coated the shaft, making it glisten in the moonlight. Kelly noticed that it had balls and could feel them against her clit when John buried it deep. She couldn't help but wonder when and where he had gotten this beautiful fake phallus. She had many toys at home, but the thought of getting one so realistic had never crossed her mind.

She whimpered when John slid it from her pussy and stood up. Kelly turned to meet his kiss. She tasted her pussy on his tongue and smelled her sweet aroma on his face.

"Look at this." John held the toy up for her to see. Kelly was amazed at how real it looked. The shaft was a creamy flesh color complete with veiny ridges. The head was rimmed with a pinkish helmet, and the balls were drawn up in a tight sack, the same way John's got right before he came. Then she noticed the suction cup on the base of the balls and the shit-eating grin on her husband's face. John reached around her and stuck it to the side of the car.

"You had this whole thing planned out didn't you?"

"Do you want to fuck a stranger and suck my cock in the abandoned lot?"

Kelly's pussy flooded at the thought. She buried her tongue in his mouth, grabbed his cock and drove two fingers in her pussy.

"Now you don't have to imagine his thick shaft, you can feel it," John whispered in her ear.

Kelly took a step back and grabbed the mythical stranger's fleshy shaft. The girth filled her hand and she let her fingers find the balls drawn tight underneath. She had no problem imagining it attached to the man in the bar. She pictured him, still wearing his jeans, but with this beautiful cock jutting through the fly.

"Can you feel him behind your?" John prodded her. "Running his hands over your ass and inside your wet cunt."

Kelly could feel the stranger's hands on her back as she leaned forward to take John into her mouth. She imagined him running his hands over her smooth ass and down to her dripping pussy.

"Do you want him to slide that big cock inside you?

"Yes."

"Do you want him to fuck your tight little pussy?"

God, John had a gift for dirty talk. His words transformed the silicone shaft in her hand, into a real man who was about to fuck her from behind. Kelly let the head slip past her lips. She stepped back and filled herself with the rigid shaft. Her inner walls quivered around it and tightened when she felt the balls touch her clit.

"How's it feel to have another man's cock filling your cunt?"

With his words Kelly began working herself back and forth on the stranger's cock. Kelly's wetness ran down the inside of her thighs. She loved the feeling of this stranger's cock filling her pussy, while her mouth ran the length of John's shaft.

She could taste the sweet and salty pre-come escaping from John; she knew this was as much of a turn on for him as it was for her. She wrapped her fingers all the way around his thick shaft and cupped his balls.

"I can see his fingers digging into your gorgeous ass as he buries that cock in your little pussy."

Kelly felt everything John was describing. She reached between her legs and grabbed the stranger's shaft, wet with her lust. She had a cock in each hand and was being penetrated from both ends. She clenched her pussy around the stranger's cock as he pushed deeper inside her.

"Are his balls slapping against your clit? I wish I could see his thick shaft spreading your slick lips. Is he going to make you come, baby? Are you going to come around his thick cock?"

She was going to come, but she wasn't ready for it yet. Kelly didn't want this to end. She had a fantastic vision of the scene in her head. She could see the stranger standing behind her. His bare chest shining with sweat as he furiously pumped her pussy. At some point John had pulled her tits out of her top and they were swaying with the motion of the stranger's thrusts.

The sexy silhouette of their threesome was clear in her mind. The glistening stranger, her taught nipples topping her swaying tits, and John's polished cock, slippery with saliva, fucking her face.

"Do you like that young hard cock pounding your pussy while I fuck your face?"

John was taking her past the point of no return. Every nerve in her body was charged and she felt an incredible orgasm building deep within.

"Where do you want it baby? Do you want him to come on your back? No, you probably want to watch his hot load squirt all over your face and tits? Do you want both of us to come on your face, to shower you in our hot sticky mess?"

The thought of two meaty cocks erupting at the same time was the catalyst for her orgasm. Kelly's pussy clamped down on the stranger's cock and she felt like she was imploding. Paralyzing energy coursed through her body and for a brief moment all of her senses became one; John's shaft sliding past her tongue, her taught nipples cooled by the passing breeze and the wetness spilling down her leg as the stranger filled her aching cunt. Kelly's body released and a feral grunt escaped her lips seconds before John exploded in her mouth.

His warm salty liquid pulsed onto her tongue. She regained control of his cock, sucking and milking with one hand while she massaged his balls with the other. She felt his body relax as she squeezed the final remnants of his orgasm down her throat.

Kelly leaned up and pulled him close, sliding her come soaked tongue in his mouth for a kiss. John pulled himself against Kelly's body. The stranger's cock was still inside her and she felt John's cock pressing against her swollen pussy from the front. She was the filling in this meaty sandwich. The vision of being smothered in flesh flashed in her mind one more time, before the stranger's cock returned to silicone.

Kelly stepped forward, letting the dildo slide from her pussy. Her body was spent and her mind was reeling with all the other places they might take the stranger. She could already picture sitting on it while John stood in front of her, sticking it to the shower wall, the possibilities were endless.

"So how was your first threesome?" John smiled.

"Holy shit that felt good. Thank you," Kelly kissed him again.

"I'm just sorry that we couldn't shower you with come at the end," John had that shit-eating grin again.

Kelly winked, "Maybe next time we should actually strike up a conversation at the bar."

TONIGHT IS FOR YOU

Autmn Tooley

Opening the door from the garage into the house, I tossed my keys in the glass bowl that sat on the counter and called out, "Grant, I'm home."

I knew he was home since his car was in the garage; but the house was completely dark except for the dancing glow from several lit candles scattered around the kitchen. "Is the power out?" I asked as I walked through the kitchen, the sharp clacking of my heels resounding on the smooth tile floor.

More candles flickered in the living room and in the wall sconces down the hall to our bedroom. "You wouldn't believe the day I've had. All I want is a pint of ice cream, a glass of wine, and bed." The faint sounds of my favorite cellist floated from the bedroom and I made my way towards the soulful sound, kicking my shoes off as I went. "Grant?"

Annoyance flashed through me at the silence; swiftly followed by concern. "Grant, are you back here?" I came through the doorway and slammed to a complete halt. Lit candles adorned every flat surface of the bedroom, bathing the bed in a rich, golden light. Rose petals pooled on the bed and off to the side, creating a delicately scented trail into the master bathroom.

Pushing open the door, Grant stood with a bottle of champagne and wearing a faded pair of button fly jeans that I loved him in. They hung low on his hips, accentuating the deep vee of his abs and the lithe build that years of running and martial arts training had honed into a supple mass of strength. My breath caught in my throat at the sight of him, a quick hitch as my lungs relearned how to work.

I licked my lips at the sight of his bare chest and felt a strong desire to run my hands over the smooth expanse of skin stretched taut over hard muscle. Seeing him without clothes always had that effect on me. Even after five years, I wanted him with a passion that knocked me on my ass. My body rooted in place and I was unable to speak as he moved towards me, a graceful predatory glide that made me think of the large cats we both liked visiting at the zoo.

Setting the bottle of champagne down, he stared into my eyes and cupped my face gently before pressing a sensual kiss to my half-parted lips. I sank into the soft caress of his lips against mine and surrendered to the teasing strokes of his tongue against my lips and opened wider to let him in. He invaded my senses and I wrapped my arms around his neck, grounding myself in him.

He eased back and trailed kisses along my jaw line until he nuzzled the hollow behind my ear. "Tonight is for you," he whispered. He stepped back and took my hand, leading me towards the giant claw foot bathtub that was the centerpiece of our bathroom. Steam rose from the milky water and the light scent of orange blossom from my favorite milk bath filled the room. Grant divested me of my clothing, his hands offering a slow, sensual caress as he tenderly stripped me. The thick silence stretched out between us, punctuated only by the soulful sounds of the cello and the intense awareness of two lovers, saying everything that needed to be said.

He held my hand as I eased into the bath and sank into the welcomed heat, and sighed. I closed my eyes and let my body relax in the hot water. A moment later, an unmistakable pop caught my attention and I cracked my eyes open in time to see Grant pouring a glass of champagne. Hunger shot through me as I watched him walk towards me and I bit my lip as temptation to peel the button fly down and slip my hand inside to release the length of him and guide him into my mouth. Desire flared in his own eyes, a liquid pool of heat that seared into me. I raised myself up in the bath. Water ran down my bare breasts and dripped off my nipples, as the sensitive buds tightened under his dark gaze. I could see the hard line of his arousal pressed into the soft faded cotton and I licked my lips in anticipation of tasting him.

He placed the glass of champagne in my outstretched hand with a knowing smile, staying just out of reach. "Sit back," he commanded, his voice husky in that way that made the muscles in my lower abdomen clench and my heart stutter. It wasn't quite a growl, but it hinted at the caged darkness that lurked inside him. I did as he said; sipping the champagne and eagerly waiting for what would come next.

Grant moved to the other end of the tub, sitting on the edge, and reached down, wrapping his large hands around one calf and gently lifting it up, resting my foot on his lap. He kneaded the tight muscles in my feet, easing the tension from spending day after day in heels. He rotated my foot at the ankle, his fingers deftly coaxing the tightness out of the joint. When my foot was pliant under his touch, he slowly worked upwards until he massaged the stress from my calf. I tipped my head back, resting on the curve of porcelain, giving in to the feel of his hands on my skin. A soft moan escaped on a sigh when he began placing kisses on each toe, nipping the pad before sucking on it and moving on to the next one.

When he finished with the first leg, he moved to the other one and the stress of the day melted underneath his sweet ministrations. I drifted on a haze of champagne and arousal, my body alive with want as his hand slipped through the water and glided along my inner thigh. I parted my legs, giving him more access and pouted when he trailed a fingertip along the crease in my thigh, avoiding my mound and the pulsing ache that was beginning to dawn between my legs.

Grant's chuckle rumbled along my breast bone and I frowned at him harder. "I'll take that," he said, reaching out to take my now empty glass and setting it down. He never took his eyes off me, and I ran my tongue along my bottom lip as I arched up, fondling my breasts. Staring at him, I plucked at my nipples and watched as his eyes flared and he took in a sharp inhale. "Minx," he scolded me before grabbing me by the hair and stretching my neck out while he kissed me hard and fierce. My hands slid up his arms until I could grip his shoulders, pulling him closer.

He broke off the kiss and gently unwound my hands from him. Taking my hand, he guided me up until I was standing and finally out of the tub. There was a warm towel hanging nearby and with quick efficiency, he wrapped it around me. He led me into the bedroom and laid me out on the bed. "Wait here," he said and then left the room. Curious at what he had planned now, I squirmed out of the towel, tossing it onto the floor, rolled over onto my side, and stretched out in a sexy pose.

My brows furrowed when Grant came back in with a tray covered with a scarf. He set the tray on the bed next to me and with a flourish removed the scrap of silk, revealing an assortment of objects: a coil of hemp rope, a crop, a leather paddle, a bottle of massage oil, and a trio of small bottles. "You can pick anything you want off the tray for me use on you." He flashed a mischievous smile and I barely contained the growing tide of need that engulfed me.

"Anything?" I asked and reached out to pick up the first of the small bottles. I flipped the top open to discover it held chocolate. I repeated the steps with the next two and found one held honey and the other strawberry syrup.

"Anything." His eyes, deep pools of heat, seared into me, and I shivered under the intensity of his gaze. It was like he saw into the very seat of my soul, finding my secrets and plucking them like juicy pieces of fruit from the tree of my darkest desires. I picked the bottle of strawberry syrup and the coil of rope and handed them to him, my hand shaking as my heart sped up with anticipation of what he would do with my selections. "Lie back and roll onto your stomach," he instructed softly, and I did as he said, turning my head to the side and tucking my hands under my cheek.

Grant ran his hands across my skin, starting at my hips and sweeping upward, letting his warm calloused palms glide lightly over my back, making my muscles twitch as he went. My back was always the most sensitive part of my body and it wasn't often that it got the attention it craved. I used to feel robbed that my breasts weren't as sensitive as my back; but in this moment, I was glad for it.

He straddled me then, trapping my body between the firm lengths of his lean thighs, the evidence of his arousal pressing into my ass. Kisses trailed up my spine. Muscles, that were once relaxed and supple, now squirmed against the delicate brush of lips against skin. It was as if thousands of butterflies fluttered around me. Every touch was a tickle of sensation that drove the need to greater heights.

The primal surge of atoms exploding and reforming accompanied the feel of teeth sinking into the back of my neck and I cried out. My arms shot out; my hands gripped the sheets; and I bucked up into him. Grant growled, and the vibration shuddered along my spine, making the inner walls of my pussy clench. He bit down harder and a delicious tension sang through my body with the sharp kiss of pain. He released me suddenly and I collapsed onto the bed, my breath coming out in heavy pants.

Grant grabbed my hands and wrapped them on the wrought iron head board, his voice a gravelly rasp in my ear. "Keep your hands on the bed frame and don't move them until I tell you to."

He left me then and I heard the familiar popping of the button fly being released. Before I could turn to watch, he crawled back on the bed, drizzling the cool liquid along my calf and quickly followed it with the wet trace of his tongue. I struggled to remain still as he continued to paint my body with the strawberry syrup, lapping it up with his tongue and occasional nibble as he nipped the back of my knee, my inner thigh, the hollow under my ass. Every touch, every lick, bite, and caress drove me to new heights and I was lost to the sea of want he was creating.

"Grant," His name escaped on a moan as his tongue delved through the cleft of my ass and along the edge of my hip. "Need something, baby?"

"You. Always you."

"Good answer." He licked his way along my ribcage and dipped low to brush the side of my breast, but the focus of his devotions was all for my back. He knew how sensitive my back was, and my skin ran hot, edgy from the climbing ache for release. I shifted under him, sawing my legs together trying to relieve the pressure that had built between them. Lost in a haze of longing, I barely registered him taking my arms from the headboard and placing them behind my back. I lay passive as Grant bound my wrists together, my breath hitching as the coarse hemp rope dragged across my sensitized skin.

"Up on your knees," he commanded and he gripped my hips, helping to steady me as I pressed my upper body into the bed and pulled my knees under me, raising my ass in the air like an offering. Grant used his body to spread my legs apart and I thrust my hips against his erection as it nestled against my core. He chuckled and gave my ass a swat. "So eager. I love that about my girl."

"Grant, please," I begged him. My body was on fire with need for him and I desperately wanted to feel him push every hard inch of him into me.

"Easy, baby. I'll take care of you." The bed dipped and Grant eased between my legs, on his back. His hands around my hips pulled me downward. I gasped as his tongue dove into my swollen folds and straight to the sensitive pearl. My body jerked as the electric sensation shot through me, my nerve endings igniting in a sharp wave of pleasure. I moaned loudly as he drove me higher towards release. His tongue made expert flicks that filled the well of pressure in my lower belly until it spilled over and I came screaming into his mouth.

He rode my orgasm out, lapping greedily as he captured the liquid honey of my release. When the last of the spasms quaked through me, Grant slipped from under me, grabbed me from behind, and slammed into my still quivering core. I arched up at his sudden invasion and Grant gripped my hair with one hand and wrapped the other arm around my waist, holding me up as he pumped into me. His thrusts hit that spot deep inside that started another gathering storm that promised to shatter me when it broke. He pulled me up by my hair until I was pressed against his chest and he thrust into me hard and fast, just the way I liked it.

His rhythm was steady and fluid, driving over that spot inside me, the friction spiraling higher and higher until he pushed me over again and my body flew apart in an orgasm so intense it was like I had slipped my skin and become pure energy. My climax sparked his own, his controlled thrusts giving way to more frenzied ones. He slammed into me hard. Once. Twice. Three times. Grant's release followed a heartbeat later and he barked out my name as he emptied himself inside me. He released his grip on my hair and wrapped his arms around me, holding me close as my body sagged into him and he sat back, bringing me with him until I was sitting on my heels, his cock still jerking inside me.

He quickly untied my arms and tossed the rope on the floor, then feathered kisses along my neck. Grant held me until he was no longer panting. He pulled out, his cock rasped across my sensitive flesh, causing me to ripple around him. He surged forward, taking me down to the bed.

He stretched out on his side and tucked me in next to him, wrapping his body around mine. I snuggled into his arms completely spent, the stress of the day forgotten. This was much better than a glass of wine and a pint of ice cream.

AFTER HOURS
Morrigan Cox

The rhythmic pulse of a drill could be heard straight through to every corner and cranny of Hangar 74. It was one thing during the day, but once the sun went down the noise should have stopped. Peggy rubbed the sleep from her eyes and moved toward the sound.

One. Two. Three. The same drone of a drill repeated again, bringing her closer to the source. The prototype room was across the hangar, but still easily to access with a quick walk.

A lone worker sat off to one side of the room, right next to a large frame with two sheets of metal clamped together. Each surge of sound marked another hole drilled through the pair of metal sheets. Rivets would be added later when there was a partner to man the backside of the sheets.

Peggy stopped just off to the side and watched her continue to drill perfectly straight holes through the metal siding. She didn't have to ask who it was once she got a good look at the distinctive curve of her backside, the rounded contours of her hips. The late-night overachiever was none other than Rose Burgess. They'd met weeks ago at a dance for the civilian workers on base.

Peggy worked with the parachutes in another part of the hangar, but she knew enough to keep out of sight when someone was drilling. One slip and the whole piece of metal had to be scrapped. No one wanted to be responsible for that kind of mistake. Outside of work, all the ladies could raise some hell, but while they were at work, they took it seriously. Just the like the Employment Service poster on the wall said, *'Do the Job He Left Behind.'*

So she waited until Rose set down the drill in favor of a marker. As Rose planned the next sequence of holes, Peggy scrambled up the scaffolding just above Rose's station.

A slight turn of her dark head said that Rose knew she had company.

Peggy dangled her legs off of the scaffolding, her calves at Rose's eye level. "You gonna stay at it all night?"

"I wasn't planning on it, but there's no rush to go home."

"Really?" Her legs disappeared and Rose heard a soft swish of sound. Leaning back on her stool, Rose squinted up into the shadows and shook her head. Peggy was lying on her stomach on the upper level, looking down over the edge. "I thought you had family around here."

"My brother when he's home, but he's somewhere in the Pacific with his unit." Rose set the drill against the clamped wall of metal sheeting and put another hole through the assembled pieces with skilled precision. Another, and then another followed until she stopped to wipe at the sweat from her forehead. "You?"

Peggy's fingers worked at the knot at the front of her kerchief, struggling with the tight wrap of cloth. "No one special." The knot gave and she pulled it off and tucked the square of fabric into the wide pocket of her jumper. "I like to flirt and horse around. I don't," she sighed, "get too serious about anyone."

Rose gave her a shrug. "My mother always told me when I meet that 'right person' then I'll know."

"That sounds vague enough that she'll always be right." Peggy watched as Rose added another few holes along the same line on the sheeting. "You've got that down."

"Even with the training, it took me awhile not to feel like I was going to go right through the whole thing like paper. Once I got a feel for it, they put me on the line. Sometimes I get into a rhythm and don't even hear the whistle."

"Which," Peggy laughed, "is why you're still here on the floor."

Rose set her drill on the rolling cart at her side, took up her rag, and wiped off the metal sheeting on the frame before her. "I should probably clock out and head home." Rose took a few steps toward the time clock and stopped, turning to face Peggy. "Why are you here so late?"

Peggy's expression tightened ever so slightly before she shrugged it off. "I was out a little late last night and when it came time for my break, I found a comfy little corner in the fabric room and curled up."

Rose nodded. "And you woke up when everyone else was leaving."

"Give me some credit," Peggy laughed outright and then winced when her cheeks colored a fetching pink. "I woke up at the whistle; I just stayed where I was until everyone left." Peggy kept the conversation moving forward, hoping to take it off of her mistake. "Have you seen the fabric room?"

"No," Rose thought about it, "but I'd like to. I've heard stories."

"Do you sew?" Peggy was eager for any information on the brunette. This was probably the longest conversation she'd had with the other woman and she wanted to keep it going as long as she could.

"Sew?" Cringing, Rose waved off the question. "I could sew a button on if it popped off, but that's about the breadth of skill that I have with a needle."

Peggy chuckled at Rose's admission. "If you're coming with me, we should make an adventure out of it." With a wink, Peggy led the way through the building, making a quick stop at the supervisor's office. She stopped Rose at the door and disappeared inside the dark room, stumbling about a bit before she returned, standing in the doorway with a bright smile and her fingers wrapped around the long glistening necks of beer bottles.

"Where did you...how did you know those would be in there?" Rose looked around, suddenly worried they'd be caught with the contraband.

The frustrated sigh that turned her head back was followed by a girlish giggle. "Hank's a bit of a flirt," Peggy explained. "He likes to think he's being subtle, and that I'll get drunk and fall into his arms."

"Why not?" Rose didn't think much about the supervisor. He was a fair man for the most part, but he'd made a few comments that didn't sit well with her when others weren't around. "Do you like him?"

Peggy handed her two of the beers, holding onto the chilled bottles as Rose's fingers wrestled with hers for a solid hold. "He's not my type, I guess." With a tilt of her head, Peggy moved them on until they were in the doorway of a room walled off from the rest of the hangar. She paused there until she was sure Rose was right behind her, close enough that she could smell the oil on her hands and feel the warmth of her body.

Rose was close enough to see the light lipstick that Peggy'd applied to her lips, and close enough to see the delicate lengths of her fingers. Maybe it was just how close they were standing, but her fingers tingled as though she was still touching Peggy's smooth skin. "So, if not Hank," she swallowed and clutched the two bottles to her chest, "have you got someone else in mind?"

Pivoting around, Peggy looked up at Rose from her lesser height. In her eyes, Rose saw a curious sparkle that reminded her of mischief.

"Yeah, someone." Peggy tipped a bottle and touched it against one of Rose's, chiming the two together like opening chord of a song. "Come on in and see."

The parachute room, as it turned out, was like a giant laundry room, with sheets of nylon hanging about like curtains or blankets waiting for the heavy touch of the sun. In a corner, Peggy explained, there was a pile of irregular fabric that had been heaped up. Peggy flopped onto the pile and gestured to Rose to follow suit. "Can't use this fabric for parachutes, we'd never know when something was going to rip apart and kill someone. Instead we sort it out and ship it to another office. Not sure what they do with it, but all the cutting and sorting certainly keeps us busy."

Rose nodded as she unscrewed the top and took a sip. Beer wasn't something she normally drank and the dry aftertaste had her sweeping her tongue around the inside of her mouth to wet it. "Busy isn't bad, I guess. Keeps me from letting my mind wonder. My brother's due to come home in a few months for R & R. I just hope he doesn't bring home another 'friend' to meet me." Another sip of beer had emptied the neck of the bottle. "I haven't taken a shine to the last dozen or so, but he keeps trying."

"Maybe you're just lookin' in the wrong place. Take me for example…"

"What other guys have you been seeing?" Rose blurted out. "Anyone on base?" She felt strange and awkward a moment later when Peggy didn't answer her question. The blackout light outside the window managed to cast some light over her face, but it dimmed the dark flame of Peggy's red hair—hair that was probably a dream to touch. "I mean," she swallowed, "not that it's any of my business, or anything."

Rose waited for a few moments, which stretched out to a few more, but she didn't revisit the question, letting it go in a silent apology to the other woman.

"Damn it." Peggy dragged her forearm over her cheek. She adjusted her position on the pile of fabric, closing some of the distance between them and turning the conversation to another track entirely. "Here I've been convincing myself that it would be cooler if they'd let us work at night."

Rose took another sip of her beer. "You thought it would be cool in here at night?" She tried, but couldn't hide her laughter.

"What?" Peggy sat up straighter and glare at the other woman. "What's so funny?"

Pressing the bottle to her neck, Rose shook her head. "You're not that far off," she explained as she used her free hand to wipe the sweat from the nape of her neck. "Maybe if they opened the windows, let in some air. Then it might be cool enough in here, but-"

"But they've got everything locked up tight." Peggy groaned out loud and flopped back against the nylon.

"Hey, watch out!"

Too late, Peggy realized that she still had the bottle in her hand, toppling it back into the filmy fabric. The two scrambled to grab the neck of the bottle and set it right, but with the two of them fighting over the slippery glass, they ended up in a tumble of limbs, laughing at their own failure.

"I'm hoping we can just wash that out later," Peggy's voice was breathless, her tone smiling.

"Sure, sure," Rose tried to sit up, but she had an arm pinned beneath Peggy's waist, "it shouldn't take long if we can hang it up to dry."

Peggy stopped moving for a moment, looking up at Rose with a wink. "Aren't you the little domestic goddess? Do a lot of washing, do you?"

The discomfort in her arm lessened and Rose gave up struggling for a moment, her eyes narrowing slightly. "Of course. You don't?"

Turning onto her side, Peggy shook her head. "No. Not if I can help it." She saw the unspoken question in Rose's eyes. "I just get my neighbor to do it for me. I buy her a bottle of something at the store and then we end up drinking it while we wait for things to dry on the line."

"So," Rose relaxed into the heady pulse of the beer again, "you mean to say you're hopeless when it comes to the wash?"

Peggy shrugged and slowly turned so her body lay flat amongst the fabric, enjoying the sensation. "Pretty much."

"Then you better let me wash your blouse." Before Peggy had the time to ask Rose what was wrong with her shirt, Rose pointed to her shoulder.

The sobering sensation only served to flatten the fabric against her skin, pulling the wet cotton flush made her meaning all too clear. The shoulder of her work shirt was soaked in beer. "Oh, damn it." Peggy scrambled to sit up, bumping her forehead into Rose's cheek. "Oh, sorry!"

Her arm freed, Rose managed to get up on all fours and then back onto her knees. "No. No worries. I should have gotten up off of you first."

"Stop apologizing for trying to help me." Peggy winced at her own tone, a little sharper than she expected. "I just didn't realize how much I'd spilled." The two shared another laugh as Peggy pulled and tugged on her hem to try to see how much of the fabric was soaked.

"Here," Rose held out her hand. "Don't try to look at it, just take it off and I'll wash it tonight and bring it back on Monday."

With such a generous offer, Peggy wasn't going to pass it up. She reached up to her neck and undid the top two buttons before grabbing the hem again and whipping her blouse over her head in one long pull.

The sudden reveal of flesh to the air made Peggy sigh with relief. "So much better, you should try it." She turned to look at Rose and froze. "What?"

Rose's eyes were focused on her. Not on her face or her middle, somewhere in between. The flutter in Peggy's middle wasn't an unfamiliar or an unwelcome feeling. In fact, after the beer she'd had and the one she'd drunk half of, she was enjoying the sensation. And seeing Rose's eyes fixed on her chest made all the cloying heat of the hangar worth every drop of sweat.

"Rose, I…"

"Where did you get that?"

The sudden question startled Peggy into a moment of silence as she struggled to gather her thoughts. "Get what?"

"That shirt."

It took another long moment for Peggy to look down. "Oh," her laughter was low and strained, embarrassment weighing heavily on her voice, "found it in the store off Main Street." Peggy raised a hand and ran her fingers along the soft cotton. "It's a knit undershirt. None of the scratchy seams and sore ruts in my shoulders from straps."

Rose smoothed her hand over her own work shirt and felt the thick seams of her brassiere stilting her movements. "I don't think I could wear something like that," she lamented with a blush, "I may not like the pinch of my longline, but I need the support and the pinch at my waist if I want to look halfway decent. It's not fun being the big cow around all of you gazelles."

"You wear that under your work clothes?" Peggy couldn't believe it. "You don't need it, sweetie."

Turning away, Rose picked up her bottle and took a long gulp of her beer, leaving it nearly half empty in her hand. "Thanks."

Peggy heard the rough scratch of Rose's voice and knew the other woman was upset. "I'm not funnin' with you, you know. I mean it." Leaving her drink behind, she scooted closer until she could tilt her head a little and look Rose square in the eyes. "You're beautiful."

"I wear a big jumper to work and drill holes and sink rivets all day. If it wasn't for the kerchief and all the hair beneath it, folks would think I was a man."

"Now you're just being mean." Peggy cuddled up closer, lifting her hand to the knot holding her kerchief tight to Rose's head. "It's easy to tell the difference," she assured her. The kerchief dropped in Rose's lap a moment later, letting loose the heavy fall of her shoulder-length hair. "Now look," before Rose could move away, Peggy's hands were sliding through her hair, twisting the silky lengths around her delicate fingers. "See?"

"You're drunk." Rose's words were tempered with her laughter. "Otherwise you wouldn't be saying those things to me."

Peggy lifted a lock of hair to her face, rubbing it along her cheek. "I'm not drunk, Rose." She opened her eyes and smiled up at the other woman. "I'm not anywhere near drunk."

She let the curled end slip through her fingers and then traced her fingers down the notched collar of Rose's work shirt, pausing when her fingertip touched the top button.

"And I want to see this get up of yours."

Rose lifted a hand, intending to still Peggy's fingers, but she felt the other woman easily fend off the attempt.

"If you aren't going to help me, Rose, then don't get in the way."

The taller woman considered it for a minute and then lowered her hand, setting it down on Peggy's shoulder instead of in her lap.

When the second button slipped free from her blouse, Rose smoothed her palm over Peggy's shoulder; the soft sweep of her flesh felt like silk under her work-roughened palm. "You're so soft."

"I'm like that all over," Peggy whispered as she worked at the buttons, freeing them faster. "I'd like to see how you feel." The last button slid free and Peggy grabbed the sides of Rose's blouse. "Will you let me, Rose?" Her eyes swept over the blush pink longline brassiere, with its fitted seams and extra length that tucked into the waist of her jumper. "Hmm?"

Drawing her plump lower lip between her teeth, Rose nodded, both afraid and desperately eager.

The shirt slid easily down Rose's arms and fell into a heap against the yards of fabric beneath them. Reaching her hands around, Peggy found the line of hooks with a practiced ease, releasing them all in quick succession. But instead of pulling the garment away in a rush, Peggy eased it forward, peeling it free of her lush curves.

As she revealed the heated flush of Rose's breasts, Peggy took her time, drawing her lips along the dark indented lines from the seams of her lingerie, and fanning her breath against Rose's tempting flesh.

When the fabric pulled away, Peggy found the pebbled tip of Rose's breast nearly pressed against her lips. She wasted no time in tasting it, her tongue laving the dark pink skin, before drawing it into the warmth of her mouth.

Rose's hands flexed as her breath seized in her lungs. Her free hand found itself fisted in Peggy's hair, half pulling and half pushing as she struggled to understand the building sensations in her body. It was only the sting of pain at the nape of Peggy's neck that pulled her mouth from sweet morsel. "Gently, love." She was only sure that Rose had heard her when the twist of hair at her nape eased and Rose gently guided her mouth to the other breast.

She gave into the silent request, enjoying the heady sensation of Rose's generous breast filling her mouth. When she felt Rose move restlessly against her, she rose up on her knees, guiding Rose onto her back. The nylon fabric beneath her molded to her skin, sticking to her shoulders as Peggy pressed Rose into the pile of raw fabric. The scent of the spilled beer reached their nostrils and made the moment more sinful than it had been.

Rose's eyes fluttered closed as she felt the wet rasp of Peggy's tongue over her sensitive flesh. "More."

And then it was over. Peggy's lips lifted from her flesh, her smiling face visible to Rose when she opened her eyes. "You want more?"

Heat flooded through her body, tingeing her naked flesh with color. "Yes."

"Then I'm going to give it to you." Peggy winked and smoothed her hands down Rose's arms, her thumbs feather light down the sides of her breasts, and down to her waist. "Lift up a little, honey."

Peggy slipped the rest of Rose's clothes down over her legs and left them piled on the floor near her feet as she worked her way back the way she came, kisses, touches, and gentle caresses along her naked skin.

The anticipation was going to kill her. Rose squeezed her eyes shut as she felt Peggy's fingertips dance up her inner thighs until she wasn't at all sure if her legs were sighing open of their own accord or if it was Peggy's tantalizing touch that had her melting.

"I love the way you feel." Peggy's voice was little more than a groan from her lips as she swept her fingers closer. "Soft," her voice was muffled slightly and Rose chanced a look.

Peggy's flame red hair was like flames licking up Rose's body as she moved. When she came to rest against Rose, their body's touching from shoulders to thighs, Peggy pressed a long deep kiss to her lips. "Let me love you, Rose."

Instead of answering her with words, Rose lifted her head, seeking Peggy's lips with hers.

The simple gesture was enough, slanting Peggy's lips against hers, feeding them both from the heat. Fingers parted her lips between her thighs, dipping within with delicious skill. A gasp fell from Rose's lips and she pushed a hand through the yards of fabric pooled around them, pressing it into her palm with the bite of her short nails. Rose drank her fill from Peggy's mouth, rocking against her body to have more of her, to feel more of her.

And the tide turned, twisted unexpectedly for Peggy. She had been sure that there was only going to be one direction to this road, but just as

Rose's body began to move beneath hers, she felt something low against her belly.

The heat of Rose's palm eased against her flesh, sliding over the slight natural swell of Peggy's belly. Having been the tutor until now, Peggy was loathe to distract Rose from her exploration. She held Rose lightly with one arm, bracing herself with her other hand, holding her breath in anticipation.

She wasn't kept waiting.

Drawing her hand down between their bodies, Rose slid her fingers through the silken tangle of curls at the crux of Peggy's thighs and let a moan fall from her lips. A wiggle of her hand slid a single finger down further, skimming over Peggy's clit and down along the slick lips of her sex.

"Oh yes," Peggy's legs parted on her throaty moan, straddling one of Rose's thighs as it lay beneath her, "yes."

"Tell me," Rose's voice was a hair above a whisper and trembling with nerves, "tell me if I'm doing it right."

Peggy could barely think and blinked down at Rose a heartbeat before she tried to speak. Two fingers pushed inside her pussy, pressing as deep as they could go, until shivers went through both of their bodies. "This feels good," Rose rotated her hand, massaging her knuckles against the slick folds of her pussy, "this feels so good."

Peggy was going to answer. She'd finally managed to string together enough words in her head to make a decent reply, but lost them a moment later when Rose lifted her head and closed her mouth over Peggy's nipple. It took both hands, fisting in the yards of nylon to keep her there, over Rose, as her friend proved a very apt and enthusiastic pupil in the art of breathless passion.

Later, lying amongst their clothes and discarded fabric, Rose smiled at Peggy, reaching up with her hand to cup the other woman's cheek in a gentle touch. "I think we may have to work after hours again tomorrow."

"I agree completely."

VENUS FLIRTING WITH JUPITER ON THE BACKSIDE OF THE CRESCENT MOON

Parker Lee

It was late; the firing had begun at dawn. The potter hung up her apron, shut down the big gas kiln, and waited for the burner flames to all sputter out. She walked through the shop, hit the fluorescents, closed the dirty French door, and stepped into the humid night. Her arms reached up in a stretch toward the tree tops and she breathed in late June air made thick with the soft sounds of chirring crickets and bull frogs calling for their mates.

High overhead, little Venus sat flirting cosmically with big Jupiter near the spine of the crescent moon, as if The Man there could not see them, and she thought immediately of the man lying naked on top of her rumpled red sheets.

A tired smile eased its way to her lips, and she inhaled the scent of the Confederate jasmine, its blooming vines climbing the walls of their arbor, the structure he'd built last year like a monument to his moving in. *Next*, he said months ago, *let's build a fire pit*. She chuckled quietly at the thought, and a stirring welled up south of her unbridled beltline. She'd always wanted a romantic man—one who could wield a hammer and lay bricks, too.

She didn't understand why this one stayed on though, why he'd chosen her to love and laugh with, to fuck and spin tales of getting hitched with. She was already sixty for gods' sake, and damn him, he still had a wife somewhere.

In the cool dark of the house, she tiptoed to the bedroom and let her clothes fall lightly to the floor. He rolled in the sack away from her, but as she crawled in, he scooted his ass toward her. Her eyes fully adjusted to the dim light of late night and sought the back of his head where unkempt hair grew just long enough in its unruly state to cover the nape of his neck. Pushing aside his coarse hair, she found the area of his strawberry birthmark, one identical to her own, and she nuzzled him there, where she'd become obsessed by the smell of his sweat and addicted to his salty taste.

She said *Hey. I love you*, and he grunted or growled, making some rudimentary noise behind closed lips. She smiled at his short-hand speech, and with her index finger, she placed lingering pressure on the crest of his seventh cervical vertebrae. His body stilled, backlit with moonlight, and she saw the meat of his cheek muscle rise in profile. He liked her little game of writing on his back in the dark.

Her paused period became a comma, streaking wag-hook designs over his spine for a few inches, and the dance became both a period pausing and a comma hooking. Her finger drew semi-colons down to the terrain of his backbone—that flat, delicious island of bone, the posterior of his pelvic bowl—and she ceased all movement, save the still, stable pressure of her pointer.

He wiggled his ass and her hand did not respond. She wondered whether he could sense the vibes of her smile tattooing his shoulder.

He wiggled again, pushing his small ass to her, wanting more attention. She imagined him hardening and growing in length.

Two breaths in, her finger moved to the sharp bone of his hip. She counted: one, two, three, and her hand cupped that bone with the same surety his palms had always given her breasts—a pulling sensation built more of sweet question than of demand.

He said *Mmm. I love you, too.*

She rocked him gently, knowing their words always worked better in short form this time of night. *I finished the firing*, she said. *Tomorrow, we get to see what's inside.*

Mmm, he said again, rolling over to face her and pulling her near. He took up her hand and placed it snug around his erection. *I only want what you've got inside.*

She eased in closer and kissed him then, ever so happy to oblige…

THE GREAT CANADIAN BEAVER EATING CONTEST
Leah Mueller

I was at Burning Man for two days before I finally looked at the official program. Up to that point, I had wandered aimlessly around the playa, scoring free alcohol, which existed in abundance. Burning Man billed itself as a radical expression of art and community, but most of its activities revolved around drinking intoxicating beverages while wearing glow-stick hats and furry knee socks. I wanted to try something new, so I swept the dust from the recycled paper schedule and opened it wide, searching for adventure.

As I scanned the pages, the words, "Great Canadian Beaver-Eating Contest, Part Deux" caught my eye. In another environment, this would have been too good to be true; but at Burning Man, where displays of public sex were common, it wasn't a surprise. Still, the vast scope of the beaver-eating project was intriguing. The members of one of the theme camps had erected a huge tent for the sole purpose of women's oral pleasure. All you had to do was show up and spread your legs. I wasn't sure what Canada had to do with this, except for its association with beavers, or what Part One had been like, but I figured that it was best to just show up and wing it.

I began the long trek across the playa, weaving a bit in the waning heat. The daytime temperatures in the Nevada desert soared well over one hundred degrees, but the nights were relatively cool, with temperatures hovering in the mid-seventies. I felt relaxed and warm in my short, green hemp mini-dress. I'd foregone underwear, figuring that it was unnecessary. I passed clusters of people on unicycles, art cars filled with screaming drunks, stoned hippies carrying didgeridoos. The layout of Burning Man was arranged in concentric circles, with each confusing arc corresponding to a different part of the body. Navigation was next to impossible.

Finally, I noted an enormous tent in the distance, with a large quantity of people standing outside. They were queued in a long line, as if waiting for a popular concert. Two men broke away from the line in disgust, and walked rapidly towards me, shaking their heads.

"Is this the Great Canadian Beaver Eating Contest?" I asked politely. One of the men glanced at me briefly, and said, "Yeah, it is. But don't bother going, it's full."

"Wow" I said. "That's a huge tent. Are you sure it's full?"

"Of course it is," the man said haughtily. He looked at his friend, and they both laughed. Then they continued their trek across the playa.

I had come a long way and I was determined. Perhaps the current inhabitants of the tent would be so satisfied that they would complete their indulgences quickly, and would vacate the tent and give other people a chance. This seemed only fair, since community was a big deal at Burning Man, as was the idea of being a participant and not a spectator. In fact, the worst thing you could call anyone was a spectator. I took my place at the end of the line and gazed at the crowd. For a group of strangers who were assembled for the unlikely purpose of giving and receiving oral sex, everyone seemed remarkably casual and relaxed. Two men dressed in dirty loincloths stood in front of me, chatting pleasantly with a dark-haired woman. The men were slightly intoxicated, and looked as though they were most likely tech workers on holiday. All three of them appeared to be about ten years younger than I was.

One of the fellows smiled invitingly at me. "There's a rumor going around that you can only enter the tent if you have a partner already" he said. "Would you like to be my partner? My name is Mark." I scanned his face and body. He was cute enough, though not my usual type. Most likely he'd been a member of a fraternity a few years earlier and he carried a reek of privilege, but I wasn't really concerned about that today. "Sure," I said, to his immense relief. "I mean, why not?"

His friend looked more sensitive, but he had already attached himself to the dark-haired woman. We exchanged pleasantries. All three of my new friends were from California, I was the sole Washingtonian. No, I had never met Kurt Cobain, I assured them. The line remained solid, refusing to alter its dimensions, even when an occasional satisfied couple emerged from the tent. Finally, Mark reached his hands around the back of my dress and began to squeeze my ass gently. "I take it that you really like it when a guy eats your pussy?" he asked. I nodded and laughed. "Well, I just love eating pussy," he said.

Under other circumstances, such an overture would have been not only presumptuous, but downright unwelcome, but we were at the Great Canadian Beaver-Eating Contest. There really was no need to wait in line for our chance in the tent. Mark and I leaned into each other, and he reached down the front of my dress, grasped my breasts firmly. "Your tits are enormous," he gasped.

I glanced over at his friend, who was still chatting earnestly with his female companion. She had sharp features, which gave her a perpetually worried expression. Her eyes darted around the crowd, finally coming to rest on a passing group of dusty hippies, all of whom carried yoga mats and flutes. "It's hard to believe that some people actually come to Burning Man for a spiritual experience," she scoffed, shaking her head.

I laughed, and we locked eyes for a moment. She was a good sort, just uptight. Mark rested one of his hands on my hip. "Let's go back to my camp," he breathed in my ear. "I'll give you the pussy licking of your life."

I'd had my pussy licked many times, by both experts and rank amateurs, so this was a bold statement. "All right," I said. Mark clasped my hand firmly and led me from the line. His friend looked anxiously at the dark-haired woman. "I guess we're going back to our camp," he said uncertainly. "Oh, I'll come with you," she replied, to his obvious relief.

The enterprising fellows had chosen to bed down for the week very close to the sex tent, so we reached their encampment in less than ten minutes. It was nothing more than a crude clump of dusty Boy Scout pup tents, with no art or theme whatsoever. A depressed-looking fellow stood in the camp's center, staring intently into a small campfire. He looked up at us with astonishment, and then his expression changed instantly to hostility.

It was apparent that the man had chosen not to accompany his two friends to the oral sex tent, thinking that it was a foolish idea because none of them would actually score. Instead, both of his friends had returned in less than an hour, each with a woman in tow. Campfire Man sank into a lawn chair and gazed furiously at the ground. "Well, that was quick," he muttered.

Sensitive Guy strode over to his tent, pulled out a bottle of wine and a stack of plastic cups. All of us poured ourselves a glass and settled down beside the fire. "Man, I promised my girlfriend that I wouldn't try to pick up anyone at Burning Man this year," Campfire Man complained. He lifted a large stick from the ground and stared at it. "What the hell was I thinking?"

"It's not a slam-dunk," the dark-haired woman said reassuringly. "Sometimes it takes a little work. One time I went to a bar, really wanting to get laid. I tried all night, but I couldn't find anyone to take me up on it."

Campfire Man glared at her with incredulity. "Jesus Christ!" he sputtered. "Women can ALWAYS get laid!" He hurled his stick violently into the fire, causing a sudden erratic storm of sparks. He settled back into the chair and his face returned to its former, sullen expression.

Of course, he had a point. If there had been a heterosexual Great Canadian Blow Job Contest, instead of one devoted to women's pleasure, it would not have been nearly as well attended. Mark reached over, slid one of his hands under my dress. "Let's go into my tent," he said. His fingers rested on the mound of my vagina and slithered downward, and I felt a strong pull in the pit of my stomach. I rose from my chair and followed Mark to his tent. The door was already unzipped, and we tumbled inside.

Gently but firmly, Mark pressed my body onto a pile of sleeping bags. He pulled the hem of my sundress upward, exposing me. I burrowed into the soft nest of blue polyester and spread my legs wide. Immediately, Mark ducked his head and went to work tickling my clitoris with his tongue. He clasped my thighs with each of his hands and worked his mouth deeper into the folds of my pussy. A thin river of his saliva ran down one of my legs and tickled my ass. I giggled involuntarily, and he stopped for a moment, looked up at me. "Is this how you like it?" he asked. I nodded, and he dipped his head again. He began to lick my clitoris with enthusiasm, while I squirmed more deeply into the layers of sleeping bags.

Mark moved his tongue rapidly, then slowed down for a few seconds to tease me, and then regained momentum. I rocked back and forth in an attempt to get his tongue to massage my clitoris more deeply. Mark's grip on my thighs became tighter and more insistent. He burrowed his face into my pussy and I felt a strong surge of new wetness. It was going to be more than easy to come—my main concern was that it not happen too soon. I pulled back slightly, and his eyes lifted.

I had always loved seeing a guy in that position—tongue working diligently on my pussy, while simultaneously looking upward at my face to make sure that I was enjoying myself. It was the utter submissiveness of the posture that always did me in. This was more pressure than I could stand, however, and my body began its release before I was able to stop it. I rolled from side to side, moaning loudly, involuntarily. Mark increased the speed of his tongue movements, going faster and faster until it seemed as though he was spinning my clitoris in circles. I came hard for a couple of minutes; ground to a gradual, shuddering halt; and then a fresh wave of orgasm began in earnest.

As the waves subsided, a small, bulging object suddenly flopped onto the floor beside me. I heard laughter, and I knew immediately that Campfire Man was having a joke at our expense. "You two enjoying yourselves?" he yelled. "I think you might need a little something to help." I quit writhing, picked up the item from the floor, and squinted at it in bewilderment. It was a condom, filled to the brim with red wine and then clumsily tied shut. A bit of liquid had leaked out, and it made a tiny crimson puddle on the floor.

Campfire Man continued to cackle loudly, but his laughter was bitter and devoid of real amusement. The poor guy was unhinged by jealousy. My pity was short-lived, however, as a second wine-filled condom sailed into the tent. Mark lifted his head from my vagina, looking annoyed. "Hey, cut it out!" he yelled, and his friend laughed even louder. "What, are you busy?" he replied.

I scooped the second condom from the floor, crawled off the pile of sleeping bags, and peered through the opening of the tent. Campfire Man stood only a few feet away, leering at me with derision. Taking careful aim, I lobbed the wine-filled condom directly into his face. "SPECTATOR!" I yelled.

The wine splattered down Campfire Man's chin and rolled onto his shirt. He stumbled backward, cursing furiously. Quickly, I retreated into the tent and zipped the door shut. Then I collapsed onto the pile of sleeping bags, laughing hysterically until I felt completely spent. Mark lay beside me, looking peevish. "I don't know why the hell my buddy is acting like that," he complained. "The asshole is always starting something." He placed one of his strong hands on my thighs, and looked into my eyes directly for the first time. "You want me to lick your pussy some more?" he offered. "I'd be glad to do it."

I inched away from the pile of sleeping bags and shook my head. "Nah, I'm good," I assured him. "That was some seriously first-rate cunnilingus." Mark smiled. "Well, I was happy to provide it," he assured me. "You sure you don't want any more?"

"It's okay," I said emphatically. "Really, thanks a lot. I think I'll be going now." Mark looked more than a bit crestfallen. "I can walk you back to your camp," he offered. "Oh, I remember the way," I said. "After all, there's no safer place in the world than the playa."

I had gotten what I had searched for, a hot and dusty reward at the end of a very difficult summer, and I was grateful to Mark for giving me pleasure without any demand for reciprocity. Usually, when sex was that good, it carried the burden of emotional involvement. My experience was completely devoid of that odious responsibility, and I felt liberated and revitalized. I had no desire to hang around in the afterglow, only to hear the inevitable tales of mortgages, shitty bosses, and evil ex-girlfriends. I gave Mark a perfunctory kiss and emerged from the tent.

The campfire was almost completely spent, but in its shadows I could make out the forms of Sensitive Guy and the dark-haired woman. They huddled next to each other in separate lawn chairs, talking intensely in low voices. Sensitive Guy was still working diligently to assure his would-be girlfriend that he would take all of her concerns into consideration. She appeared dubious. Campfire Man had vanished completely. Perhaps he had retired to his tent or he maybe he had decided to take his chances on the roulette wheel of the oral sex tent, after all. Most likely, he didn't even have a girlfriend to worry about.

I wished them all luck and began my trek across the sands to where my tent awaited me—my oasis amongst thousands of other temporary resting places that were spread densely across a minute portion of the Nevada desert. A slight, welcome breeze blew up the bottom of my dress and tickled my pussy. The Man would burn in two more days, and the next night the Temple, and then it would finally be Labor Day—time to pack everything and go home.

INK

Sophia Soror

It started with a smile when we passed each other at the top of the gangplank. As he stepped aside to let me pass, I felt him sizing me up; admiring the cut of my dress and the curves of my figure. I had left not an inch of skin showing that wasn't face or hands, but the way my dress clung to my body left nothing to the imagination. The effect it had on this man was a stare that followed me to the bar and crept under my skin, sparking long-dormant appetites. I watched him go from the corner of my eye, a little disappointed he hadn't followed me, but I had friends to attend to. Amy and Sarah were standing by the hatch, looking antsy.

"Finally here," I announced. "How's Diane holding up?"

"I think she's got stage fright," Sarah said. "I've already taken her two glasses of wine to calm her down. Big ones."

Amy snorted. "Will she be able to read without falling over?"

A server came by with my drink. "It's her first book," I said. "Of course she's nervous. It's like offering yourself up as a virgin sacrifice."

My friends continued speculating over Diane's performance and I tuned them out, preferring to explore my surroundings. Diane had been adamant that she wanted the launch of *Nemo's Wife* to take place on a boat. The asking price to hire the hundred-year-old tallship sitting out in Elliott Bay was a bit steep, but I was more than happy to chip in. For the chance to spend an evening on the *Adventuress*, I'd have sold my left ovary.

"We should get below," Amy said. "She starts in five."

Sarah snorted. "If she's not in the bathroom puking."

"Head," I corrected.

"Huh?"

"We're on a boat. It's called the head."

"Yeah thanks, show-off."

I waited for my friends to descend below decks before I followed. I scanned the faces of the partygoers one more time, but didn't spot the one smile I was looking for. Disappointed, I headed down the ladder.

Diane's reading was well applauded at the finish. Almost before the Q&A had finished, people were already climbing out of the confines of the aft cabin. Even I was clambering for fresh air by the time she was done.

During the reading, tall tables with white clothes and candles had been set up along the dock. We disembarked the vessel and took the table of honor with the author, trying to keep ourselves amused while guests flattered Diane with compliments.

I hadn't been standing there long when a gin and tonic I didn't order arrived at our table. On the napkin was scrawled "Murphy," nothing else. I stopped the waiter as he started to walk away.

"I'm sorry, I won't be accepting this."

"Oh come on," Amy complained. "For once, just accept the damn drink. Who's it from?"

The waiter pointed. Standing at the foot of the gangplank was the smile I'd been thinking about for the last hour. Dark hair fell into eyes distinguished by deep laugh lines. When he saw me look over he straightened, lifted his glass, and drank to me. Those green eyes never left mine. Oh hell, and why not? I hadn't bothered with men since my last breakup, and that had been sometime last year. And it felt good to feel desired.

"Think you can do without me for a while, ladies?"

Sarah looked over. "Him? Jesus, he looks like he wants to swallow you whole."

"If anyone does any swallowing, I doubt it'll be him."

I picked up the glass and its napkin, put a sultry sway in my hips, and walked over. I watched him watch me as I walked right on past him and up the gangplank, back onto the ship. I felt his gaze hot on the back of my neck and in the tingle of my thighs. His footsteps were soft behind me as I went aft and took up position by the rail. Only a few people remained on board, and back here all was quiet. I leaned against the rail, looking out at the lights of the West Seattle peninsula.

"Lovely view," he said behind me and I turned.

"You must be Murry."

"Is my handwriting that bad?"

"Not particularly. It's a pleasure to meet you, Murphy."

"Likewise, Miss…"

"Miranda Minh."

"Murphy and Miranda. It has a nice ring to it." He took my hand and raised it to his mouth. His lips brushed my fingers, his warm breath ghosting over my skin. Again he refused to drop his gaze and I saw something in it that would eagerly devour me. And I would have been happy to let it.

"Where's your date?" I asked.

"What date?"

"Diane's book is geared toward a more…female demographic. I can't imagine you came on your own."

"Hey, it's a party on a century-old schooner and a book about ships. How could I resist?"

"Yeah, but it's kind of a romance."

Murphy shrugged. "Even I had a bit of a crush on James Mason as Nemo when I was a kid." He leaned in. "Is this your way of asking if I'm seeing anyone?"

"Of course not. I've only just met you."

"And I don't need to ask if you're seeing anyone."

"Oh?"

"Any man who leaves you hanging when you walk out the door looking this incredible is an ass."

"Keep laying on the flattery and I'll start thinking you're after something."

"Aren't we both?"

He took a drink from his beer and I noticed, just below his thumb, an anchor tattooed in white.

"This?" he said when I asked him about it. "'Murphy' means 'Sea-warrior.'" He took my hand again and ran his fingers over the tiny star tattooed between the thumb and forefinger of my palm. "And this?"

"A tradition in British ports," I said. "A guiding star for sailors to follow home."

"How compassionate of you to guide lost vessels into your port."

"What can I say? I have a soft spot in my heart for seamen." He grinned as he continued to circle the star on my hand with his fingertips, then wandered over my wrist and further up my arm. His touch tickled through the knit of my gown and it sent shivers through my body. A flush crept up my neck and down through my belly, dampening my thighs. My bra chafed over my suddenly stiff nipples.

"Any other tattoos I should know about?" he asked.

"I'd have to undress to show you."

"Promise?"

Part of me was tempted, at least as a little tease. I could let him unzip my dress just enough to give him a peak at the lines and whorls that patterned my back. He was watching me decide, tonguing his lower lip, but I just smiled at him.

"Ask me again later."

"Unfortunately for me, it will have to be much later. It's getting late and I have a double shift tomorrow. But I have my day off on Monday. Would you let me take you to dinner?"

"Of course," I said, forgetting to play coy. I set down my drink to get one of my cards from my clutch and handed it to him. Of course I would have preferred to fuck him senseless in the galley, but this way I would see him again after tonight. He'd piqued my curiosity with his anchor tattoo and love of old ships.

"I'll call you tomorrow on my break." He brushed an escapee strand of hair back behind my ear and his eyes fell down to where his thumb dragged across my lower lip. "Would you mind if I kissed you goodnight?"

"Please," I said, and he bent down. His was not the hungry, lust-fueled kiss I had expected, but chaste; soft and lingering.

"Goodnight, Miranda," he whispered into my mouth, then was gone. I watched him make his way down the gangplank, throwing a last look over his shoulder, and back up the dock. My friends, still at the author's table, watched him go, and then turned to me with several emphatic gestures indicating that I should go after him. I shook my head and turned back to the water. I wanted to enjoy the quiet a little while longer, just me and the ship. The salty air should have made me shiver, even at this time of year, but my skin burned. I lost myself for a while, staring out at the water and imagining the feel of large hands and warm lips. I could even fancy that I heard the way he spoke my name.

A man's body pressed me against the railing, hands around my waist. "Miranda," he said again. A whisper. A prayer. He turned me around. Murphy's hair was even messier than it had been, as if he'd been running his fingers through it.

"I couldn't wait until Monday night," he said as he traced my cheekbone with his thumb. I could feel his desire against my stomach.

"For what?"

"To kiss you again." He pressed his lips first to the corner of mine, breathing me in, and again just under my ear, making me shake. He kissed a line down my neck before he took my mouth with force and a sharp intake of breath. His hands clutched my dress and my fingers knotted in his hair as we tasted one another, sharing each other's breath.

"Until Monday," he said when he drew back, and was gone again.

I was a little shaky on my legs as I made my way down the gangplank, but after careful progress, I made it safely back to my friends.

"Who the hell was he?"

"Did you get his number?"

"Why is your face so red?"

"Are you going to see him again?"

"You look like you could use another drink. Where's the one you had?"

I held up my hands against the inquisition. "I'll tell you about it later." I took a sip from a tepid glass of water and grimaced. Down here the lights were too garish and the people too loud. The heat in my skin and my thighs started to ebb and my teeth were on edge.

"I'm calling it a night, ladies. See you tomorrow." I practically ran back to my car. I just wanted to be home. When I finally gasped out my climax in the small hours of the morning, the name my pillow heard was "Murphy."

Our first date did nothing to release the pressure building in me. My want wound tighter every minute we spent together. We spent dinner getting to know one another, not just trading innuendos and struggling to keep our clothes on. He was fascinated by my job as a coroner's assistant and the stories I told about my grandfather, a merchant sea captain originally from Phú Quý. I tried not to raise my eyebrow when he told me he was a registered nurse. He'd started out in pre-med, but soon realized that nurses are the ones that actually help people. That compassion endeared him to me.

When he dropped me off at my apartment, he did not invite himself up, just kissed me and walked back to his car. His kiss had lost none of its potency and I wrapped myself up in the heat of his mouth and the subtle musk of his cologne. I'd find no satisfaction with my vibrator that night, nor after our next two dates.

On our fourth date he, took me to a tiny little restaurant I'd never heard of in Belltown. It was in an old wine cellar and when we reached the bottom of the stairs, we found ourselves in a long, narrow room of dim lighting, raw brick walls, and hardwood floors. The only tables were a single line of private booths, quiet and secluded. The maître d' showed us to one at the end.

"You're quiet tonight," I said after we ordered. "Everything alright?"

Murphy just smiled warmly at me, his fingers ghosting over the back of my hand and circling the tattoo on my palm. After a minute he dug in his coat pocket and produced a slender box wrapped in blue paper, pushing it towards me with only a hint of hesitation.

"What's this for?" I asked as I opened it. Inside was a single pearl in a silver setting. "Oh Murphy…"

"Do you like it?"

"It's beautiful." He came to my side of the booth and I turned away to let him put the delicate chain around my neck.

"One month ago today," he said, "I met the woman who would undo me."

"You keep track of that kind of thing?"

"Have it written on my calendar and everything."

"So this is like an anniversary present."

"The first of many, I hope." He finished clasping the chain and trailed his fingers down my arm and back up my spine. "You enrapture me, Miranda," he whispered, lips close behind my ear. Heat radiated off his body and into mine and his breath made the wisps of my hair tickle my neck.

Murphy bowed his head and kissed my shoulder, moving the strap of my dress aside. His lips traveled up my neck, lingering against my skin at each pause. The lines of my ink were traced with his tongue until his teeth tugged at my earlobe. His breath and my own pulse filled my ears. I started to turn to him and his hand went immediately behind my neck, pulling my mouth up to his. The cold bricks of the wall at my back made me shiver against the heat of his tongue and I gripped the collar of his shirt to pull him into me.

"Keep kissing me like that," I said as I stopped to catch my breath, "and we might not make it back to my apartment."

"And what would you do?" he asked, taking my lips again. "Drag me out by my tie and have your wicked way with me in the backseat of my car?"

"There are all sorts of things I could do to you on this table. Especially if we're using your tie around anything other than your neck."

He grinned. "You're a bit of an exhibitionist, aren't you? Or are you all talk?"

"Is that a challenge?" I asked. He stared at me a moment, searching my face for a flicker of fear but I wouldn't betray my doubt. I'd never had the guts to fuck in a public place before, but waiting for a month for Murphy to touch me made me bold. His hand moved up my thigh, taking the hem of my skirt with it. As the fabric uncovered my stockings he took a sudden interest in the suggestion of pattern underneath.

"What is this, a fish tail? How far up does this go?"

"I can show you later."

"More promises."

His fingers explored. The lightest touch inside my thigh made my legs widen involuntarily and my stomach clench. He delved higher and I grabbed his hand.

"Please," I whispered.

"Please stop? Or please more?" I didn't answer. I wasn't sure.

Lifting my chin so I would meet his eye, he raised two of his fingers to his mouth and sucked them until they glistened.

He hadn't needed to wet his fingers before he slid them into me. I'd been wet for him since that first smile, and he knew it. He was a damn tease. He curled his fingers and the shock made my body arch, thrusting against his hand. My mouth opened for a moan but I bit it back. He watched me, watched every flicker that passed over my face, eagerly drinking in the ecstasy he gave me.

His thumb found my clit and I gripped his shirt. He held me there, pinned between the wall and his body, his fingers fucking me and his thumb winding merciless circles around my clit. His breath was ragged in my ear, hot against my neck. His teeth grazed the edge of my jaw before he bit down on my earlobe and an audible gasp ripped from my throat. I didn't care if people could hear me. I held him tight against me, feeling my orgasm building.

"Not yet," he whispered into my ear and withdrew, leaving me empty, gasping, and frustrated. I had to take a few gulps of water before I could speak.

"You are a cruel man, Murphy." Grinning, he raised his hand to his mouth and sucked his still-wet fingers. "Murphy." I grabbed a fistful of his hair and pulled him to me. I wanted to know how I tasted to him. I was starving for him.

We didn't bother with dinner. We had it boxed up before it reached our table.

At the security door of my apartment building, I could barely punch in the code. He was determined to kiss me every moment he could.

"Come inside," I said.

"With pleasure."

Upstairs, I had barely fit the key in the door before his hands slid up the back of my thighs, fingers hooked under the straps of my garter belt, and lifted my dress over my ass. His grip pulled my hips back and his arousal pressed against me, cosseted between my cheeks. My hands shook so badly that I fumbled with the lock. I should have cared that someone might have caught us. I entertained the idea of letting him fuck me like that right there in the hall, hands braced against the door of my apartment. But the lock clicked and swung open, and we tumbled into the dark. His mouth was on mine before the door had even shut and his hands were unzipping my dress. The rising tide of desperation that had been churning in me since he'd sent me that first drink and the napkin with his name on it was screaming like a siren in my blood.

"Show me," he whispered. "Keep your promises."

I led him into the living room and flicked on the lights. The air felt chilly on my skin and my nipples tightened when I removed my bra. My breasts fell heavy against my ribcage, aching for Murphy's hands. Hooking my thumbs under my garter belt I bent down and shimmied out of my nylons. I wanted to feel his eyes devour me. He motioned for me to turn and I spun on the spot, displaying myself proudly before him. Over the years my body had become my canvas, and the main attraction stretched her figure down my side and over my hip, wrapping her tail in a spiral down my leg. Her hair fanned across my back, patterning ships and serpents from her curls.

"A siren?" Murphy asked, peeling off the rest of his shirt as he approached. He wrapped his tie around his wrist.

"A mermaid," I said.

"I see. Don't mermaids save drowning sailors?" He nibbled the guiding star on my hand.

"If we're appeased. If not, we may whip up a tempest to break ships and drag sailors with us into the deeps."

"And are you going to save or sink my ship?"

I ran my hands over his chest and the patch of dark ink on his left peck; a two-masted schooner with the name *Equator* scrawled under it.

"I might steer you safely to port. Then again, I might pull you into the abyss and devour you."

"Turn around," he said, his voice raspy. I obeyed and bent slightly to give him a better look, resting my hands on the arm of my couch. Silk touched my face as he draped his tie over my eyes and tied it at the nape of my neck. In the darkness I could feel his breath, fast and ragged against the back of my neck. A sharp tug at my hair made my hips bucked forward against the arm of the sofa. The fabric was rough against my already sensitive sex; a stark contrast to the silk of the blindfold.

Murphy had taken out my clip and his fingers eased my hair from its tight coil, cascading down my back in waves and breaking across my buttocks. Something like a growl in his throat was followed by the unmistakable sound of a zipper, fabric on skin, and the crinkle of a condom wrapper.

The chilly air of my apartment made his hands all the warmer as they explored the mermaid's body that had been inked onto mine. His nails raked down my back and his grip left fingerprints on my hips. The tip of his cock nudged between my thighs and pressed against me. Every nerve in my body jolted as it rubbed against my clit. Murphy kicked my feet wider apart and pulled my hips sharply back, piercing me with just the head of his cock. I tried to push back and take in more of him, but he held me firm and withdrew, leaving me with a hollow ache. One hand slid up my spine to the back of my neck and fisted my hair, pulling my head sharply back and ripping a moan from my throat. He pressed in again and I dug my nails into the upholstery, waiting for him to stretch me further.

"Stop teasing me, Murphy," I growled. In an instant, I was straddling him on the sofa. He wrapped my limbs around him and lifted my hips until I felt the tip of his mast once more against my slit. With agonizing slowness he lowered me onto him, every nerve in my body firing as I felt him ease deeper into me. Need crackled under my skin and pooled in my belly, boiling my blood. Murphy crushed me against him when I was seated fully, arms tight around me. He rocked his hips upward and I moved against him in unison, steady at first as we adjusted to the each other's bodies. My lover clung to me, face pressed into my neck, mouth at my throat. I took control, thrusting hard against him in a frantic pace and feeling him shudder beneath me. His hands found my face and tore aside the blindfold, forcing me to look down into his green-eyed gaze. It flooded through me and gripped me hard, harder than his arms around me or the thrust of his cock against that sweet spot I so loved. Blood rushed in my ears accompanied by the slap of skin. Still he never dropped his gaze from mine, but devoured every gasp and every drop of sweat as our orgasm broke over us. I felt more than heard my name on his lips as we slowed the rocking of our bodies into a gentle sway and finally calmed to an easy stillness.

We sank into the sofa, bodies wrecked and spent, throats parched. Neither of us said anything as we waited for our pulse and breath to slow. I shifted in Murphy's arms so I could lay my head on his sweat-drenched chest and listen to the pounding of his heart. Any artful comment I'd hoped to make had drowned in the aftermath of our tempest and I was left shivering. I wished he'd just say something, anything, but the only sound from him was the shudder of his breath. I traced his ship tattoo as it rose and fell.

"Miranda," I looked up at him when he whispered my name. Two green irises looked back at me, one with a dark mote like a drop of ink in my lover's eye. He tickled my forehead with his lips, then took my hand and pressed my palm to his mouth, caressing my guiding star.

"So did I steer you home safe?" I asked.

He kissed me, slow and deep. "My home is in the abyss with you."

INTRO TO RELIGION AT THE GENIAL WORT
Paul Henry

"You prostituted yourself to many shepherds and then you returned to me."
—Jeremiah 3:1

Assistant Professor Marianne Van Diemen's late afternoon, pre-tenure hearing had not gone well. Now, still seething, and clearly in a predatory mood, Van stepped brashly through the stainless steel doors of the Genial Wort Brew Pub & Cafe. *"The dean can't see past my nose,"* she fumed.

A forty-something slub in a bad suit stared at her legs from his stool at the bar. The three-inch heels of her Edmundo Castillo sandals swept his eyes from her ankles, down the transparent straps to her toes. She'd paid $400 for the sandals at Bergdorf's, probably twice the price her admirer paid for his suit at Men's Warehouse. *"Maybe he's a CPA,"* she thought. *"I could get 'audited' tonight."*

As Van approached the red-haired businessman, his eyes moved up her legs to her tiny white pleated skirt. Van paused to adjust the Prada purse strap as his eyes moved to the base of her red halter-top. He didn't see her nose until she reached the bar.

"May I join you," she asked, easing into the stool beside him.

"I'm waiting for someone," he said nervously.

"No problem." She stood to leave.

"No, it's not like that. It's a guy...."

"Oh," she said, in mock disappointment.

"No! Not that either." His face flushed with embarrassment. "He's my brother-in-law."

"So you're a married man?" She sat back down on the stool. "Pity." The bartender set a cold pint of St. Augustine IPA in front of her. "Thank you, Jeremiah." She brushed her right hand lightly across the bartender's arm. He smiled. Van crossed her legs and extended her hand to the businessman. "I'm Van."

"Skip," he said, his eyes drawn back to her amazing feet.

"Charmed."

"Van," he asked, staring at her toe cleavage, "are you a working woman?"

"Of course. How can a single girl keep herself in quality footwear without gainful employment?"

"No," he said, lowering his voice, "I mean are you a working woman?" The fingers of Skip's right hand splayed out toward her toes.

"Worse than that," Van whispered, brushing against his leg, "I'm a religion professor."

The slub sat up straight in his chair. "The Religion Department lets you dress like this?"

"There's no dress code for New Testament scholars," she said, running her fingers from his shoulder down to his left hand, pausing at his wedding band. "A woman doesn't have to be the Virgin Mary to teach divinity."

"She shouldn't be Mary Magdalene!"

"Magdalene wasn't a whore." Skip caught a nipple flash as she gestured in the loose-fitting halter-top. "Pay attention," she scolded, lifting his chin to force eye contact. "In Jewish law, only a woman's husband was allowed to see her hair undone. That's why everyone was scandalized when Magdalene let her hair down for Jesus." Van sipped from her IPA. "She just saw him as husband material."

"I have no clue what you're saying," Skip said shaking his head.

"Maybe another beer will help?"

"It's worth a try." Skip raised his empty bottle of Bud Light. "A little service." He waved the bottle in the Jeremiah's direction.

Van grabbed his hand. "Skip, don't embarrass yourself. Look at what you're drinking." She took the bottle from him. "The Genial Wort produces the best craft beers in Wisconsin." She pointed to the bartender delivering pints of amber ale to a pair of twins in matching Capri pants and pastel cashmere sweaters. "When you order Bud Light, you tell the world you don't know shit about beer."

"And I suppose you do?" As soon as he said it, Skip realized that she did.

"I know a lot of things." Van ran her fingers through her long brown hair. He caught another flash of nipple.

Skip shifted on the bar stool, attempting to adjust his wayward penis now standing at full attention. A condensed New Testament rested in his suit jacket pocket from this morning's Bible study breakfast. "Do you know about sin?" he asked.

Van raised her perfect eyebrows. "I have more than a passing knowledge of the subject." She paused. "Did you study Greek in college?"

"I was a finance major."

"I'll take that as a 'no.'" Van wasn't sure Skip was worth the trouble, but she explained anyway. "People erroneously translate the Greek word 'hamartia' as 'sin.' The term originated in archery. It meant simply 'to miss the mark.' Some nights, Skip, I'm a bad marksman." She stroked his arm. "Tonight I feel especially bad." Skip began breathing through his mouth.

Van's halter-top was formed by two wide strips of red satin joined by three small silver chains that created a two-inch gap from her waist to her breasts. At her breasts, the straps diverged and disappeared behind her neck. Skip stared at her bare shoulders. She had freckles. "Do you always dress like this?"

"Only when I want to make a statement." Van smiled a six-years-of-orthodontia smile. "Tell me, Skip, what statement does this dress make?"

Skip licked his dry lips. He really needed another beer. "'Fuck me.' That dress says, 'Fuck me.'"

"Close enough." Van crossed her legs causing the short pleated skirt to ride up her thighs, exposing the tops of her nylons. "You up to it?" She began rocking her leg slightly, teasing the skirt up further and flashing her red garters.

Skip stared a long time. He swallowed hard. "I have to pass. Thanks anyway." He turned back to the bar and focused on his empty beer bottle.

Van, too, turned back toward the bar, but leaned slightly in Skip's direction, her nipples on display. "What part of 'Fuck me' don't you like?"

She brushed her hand across his inner thigh. He jumped. He tried to focus, but she'd begun stroking the front of his pants. He was larger and thicker than she'd imagined.

"It's the nose," he moaned.

"I have other assets," she purred, varying the speed and force of her strokes, bearing down on his cock as his breathing quickened.

"Your nose is huge…!" He shifted his focus, "But … your legs are … amazing, and your toes...!" The sight of her toe cleavage took him over the edge. He came in three bursts of cum, soaking his jockey shorts and dampening the front of his suit pants.

Van smiled and stopped rubbing. She leaned back and wiped her right hand on a napkin. Then she took a long, cold satisfying drink of St. Augustine Ale. "When I peel off this dress, it won't be my nose you'll focus on."

Skip's nodded. She was probably right. He hadn't come like that in a long time. His heavy breathing slowed. He looked at the damp spot on the front of his suit pants. "What will my brother-in-law think?"

Van laughed. "He could watch."

Skip tried to visualize it. "I'm afraid that would take a lot more beer."

Van looked around the bar. Slim pickings tonight. Skip appeared to be the best prospect among a bad lot. "I'll buy the next round," she said. "But let me get you a decent beer."

Jeremiah magically appeared. "Another IPA, Van?" he asked wearily.

"Please." She leaned forward flashing her breasts. "It's a chilly night." Van motioned to Skip. "And I want something to loosen up my new best friend. Bring him a Happy Day Pils."

Van and Jeremiah's relationship was a comfortable friendship carefully crafted over hours of conversation at the bar. They'd been able to avoid the traps inherent in a sexual relationship, provided they didn't count the quickie in the ladies room on Halloween night, three weeks earlier. She'd come to the Genial Wort Costume Party dressed as a ghoulish Greek Jocasta. The noose she'd hung herself with still wrapped around her neck, her soiled white gown was diaphanous and revealing.

Knowing Van's plans, Jeremiah dressed as Oedipus, complete with fake blood dripping from his damaged eyes. They'd determined that their frenzied coupling was fated by the gods, but it ended too quickly because a line was forming to use the ladies bathroom that they'd occupied. Then things got complicated. Jeremiah was scheduled to close, and Van accepted an invitation to another party by three firefighters dressed as Musketeers.

Van screwed the Musketeers jointly and in pairs, but left the party with the Bee Gees cover band after their last set. Neither she nor Jeremiah ever spoke about Halloween night.

"What's a pils?" Skip asked.

"A pilsner." Van patted his leg. "Don't trouble yourself with the beer order, darling." Skip surrendered his empty bottle of Bud Light.

As Jeremiah eased away he whispered, "You could do better." Van knew he was right.

She glanced at her reflection in the mirror that lined the bar. She was flushed, excited, and definitely damp, not so much from the prospect of leaving with Skip, as from the look of jealousy she saw in Jeremiah's eyes. Then she saw her nose. Giant. Unmistakable. Hooked. And she wondered if she really could do better.

Skip's eyes drifted back to her toes. "I'm not comfortable with this religion professor thing," he said.

Van stopped unbuckling his belt and put her hands firmly on the bar. "Well, I'm not comfortable with this 'married' thing." Jeremiah brought their pints of beer. Van pushed the pils over to Skip, and picked up the IPA. "Is your brother-in-law married?"

"Divorced."

"Terrific." She breathed in the hops as she lifted the beer glass to her lips. "Is he in business, too?"

"Academics."

"Maybe I'll give him a try." That comment got the reaction from Jeremiah that she had predicted. He walked away.

In the mirror Van could see Skip pouting. "You know, this is all about *concupiscentia carnis*."

"What?"

She turned to face him. "Fleshly desire. You've got it. I've got it. But we also have free will." As Van sipped the beer a thin layer of foam appeared on her upper lip. "I can control my desire. Sometimes, I choose not to. How about you?"

Skip's eyes drifted down her legs to her toes again. He imagined what it would be like to suck them. He'd rip away her nylons with his teeth, then lick and stroke the gap between each toe as she squirmed in ecstasy, driving her mad with desire as he sucked each toe, beginning with the smallest, until the five of them filled his mouth. He could taste them already and he was hard again. He made a decision. "Stay right here. I need to take a whiz."

"Go crazy." Van watched Skip disappear into the men's room as she drank in the bitterness of the IPA.

That's when Van felt a tap on her left shoulder. "Can I buy a lady a beer?" She looked up at a bear of a man, early twenties, in a black t-shirt. She hadn't noticed him in the bar earlier. She recognized him as the starting offensive center for the Fighting Ospreys. Van scrupulously avoided liaisons with students, but after her meeting with the Welfare Committee today, it probably didn't matter. She wasn't getting tenure. And Skip was unlikely to satisfy her.

"Who told you I was a lady?" she asked coyly. The bear grinned broadly, leering at her through his beer goggles. Her nose would not be a problem. She pivoted on the bar stool until her leg was firmly pressed against him. "My name is Van." She stroked his tattooed arm.

"Van?"

"He's capable of speech," she thought. *"That's a plus."*

"It's short for Van Diemen. That's my last name."

"There's a professor at the college by that name."

"That's what people tell me."

Van watched him follow the line of bare skin down to the small white skirt. "You got a first name?" he asked. He placed his gigantic hand on her thigh. His palms were sweating.

"I don't use my first name. How about you?"

"Huh?" He began pawing her leg.

"Do you have a name?" she asked as his left hand disappeared under her skirt. Van clamped her legs together and spoke very slowly. "What ... is ... your ... name?"

"Chet."

"Now we're making progress. Tell me, Chet, what's your view on original sin?"

"Is that a trick question?"

"It's relevant. Original sin, Chet?"

"I'm for it."

Van drank deeply. She wasn't drunk enough for this conversation. She tried again. "In his *Confessions*, Augustine said ordinary people (like you and me) lack the strength to resist sin." She set her glass down. "He believed we couldn't control our sexual impulses. What do you think?"

Chet looked at the beer glistening on Van's lips. "Am I going to get laid or not?"

"That hangs in the balance, my little theological ignoramus."

Chet looked at the name etched on the beer glass. "Genital Wart. What kind of name is that?"

"Don't say another word." Van put a finger to his lips. "You are unbelievably stupid."

"That's cruel, ma'am."

"The name is Genial Wort. 'Genial' means having a good-natured disposition. You, I suspect, could be very genial." Chet smiled. "'Wort' is the sugary liquid produced when crushed malted grain and water are added to yeast and hops."

Before Chet could respond, another football player appeared at the bar wearing a baseball hat that read Cocks. He slapped Chet on the shoulder. "Hey, good buddy, I thought we were playing pool." Van pulled Chet's hand from between her legs and adjusted her skirt. "Well, hello Professor Van Diemen," said the jock. "I didn't recognize you without your briefcase."

"Professor?" Chet asked. "You know her, Bob?"

"She's the cunt who flunked me for lifting the paper on Martin Luther." Bob moved in on Van. "You know, if you'd dressed like this for class, I would have *come* more often."

Van reached for her purse.

Bob blocked her way. "You need another drink."

"Mr. Markum, I can't be bought for a bucket of Coors and a platter of hot wings. Try Ladies Night at the Thirsty Beaver." As she started to stand, Bob clamped a meaty hand on her shoulder.

"You've got a big honking nose and tiny tits," Bob said, forcing her back onto the stool, "but I like the dress." He eased onto the stool next to Van, tightening his grip on her shoulder. "So, I'm buying you a beer, bitch." Bob gasped and grimaced as Van seized the bulge in his pants. She clamped down. She twisted. As Bob reached for her neck, a hand tapped his shoulder. He hesitated.

"The lady doesn't welcome your advances."

Bob looked at the newcomer.

"Dean Fortis!" Chet said.

The dean acknowledged the two football players. "Is there a problem?"

Bob moaned when Van released his private parts. She pulled at her skirt to restore decorum. "Mr. Markum and I had a misunderstanding about the propriety of purchasing an alcoholic beverage for a faculty member."

"I see. Is that an accurate summary of events?" he asked the boys. Bob nodded, leaning on Chet for assistance. "Perhaps you boys should call it a night since the playoffs are this weekend."

"It's my birthday, Dean Fortis," Chet explained. "We're celebrating." He turned to Van. "Pleased to make your acquaintance Professor Van Diemen." He took a last look at her legs and the tiny white skirt. He sighed and then dragged Bob away. He wasn't getting laid tonight—at least not by Van.

Van glared at the Dean. "What are you doing here?"

"I'm not stalking you, if that's what you're suggesting. I'm meeting someone."

Her heart sank. "Skip?"

"How did you know?"

"I made his acquaintance a little earlier." She motioned to empty stool beside her.

Dean Fortis sat down. He loosened his tie. "Didn't Isaiah write, 'You spread your legs in every alley and wasted your beauty'?"

"It was Ezekiel. Ezekiel 16:23-24, but good try."

The Dean motioned to Jeremiah for a beer, ignoring her remark. "You know, Professor Van Diemen, if you stopped dressing like a whore, people would stop mistaking you for one."

"That wasn't exactly the prophet's point, but close enough." Jeremiah appeared with two fresh IPAs. Van mouthed the words, *Thank you*, and the bartender disappeared. She pushed one of the pints to the Dean and lifted the other. "The Religion Department hates me, you know."

The dean lifted his glass, caught the aroma of the hops, sipped tentatively, and then embraced the beer. "The Religion Department is a den of vipers."

"Vipers?"

"Yes. The whole campus knows that. If the Religion Department liked you, then you'd be in trouble." The dean's eyes wandered to where the tiny skirt had risen on her thighs. "The Welfare Committee is sympathetic to your situation. And they are impressed by your *publications*."

Van ignored his stares. "My students hate it when I question their religion. They feel threatened, so my evaluations are in the crapper."

"True," the dean acknowledged, "but your student evaluations are superior to those of the tenured members of your department who teach similar classes." He wondered what it would feel like to have those legs wrapped around his waist as he entered her.

Van recognized the look in the dean's eyes. She swiveled on the bar stool to face him. "I didn't know that."

"Your department chair should have told you. The evaluation process is a comparative."

She uncrossed her legs. "My Jesus seminar got rave reviews last spring." She demurely sipped the IPA and slowly began to spread her legs.

"That it did." He lowered his beer to the bar and moved into the space opened by her legs.

"What's your take on Augustine?" she asked as she drew him into her.

"He was very negative on matters of the flesh." He reached under her thigh with his left hand. "I don't share his opinion."

She moaned softly as she guided his hand to its destination. "I'm so glad to hear that." She drew her right leg up and rested her foot on his stomach. Her tiny white skirt slipped up to her waist, revealing her red garters and white satin panties. "Augustine felt the problem was the sperm," she said.

"Sperm?" The dean grabbed her ass cheek to retain his balance. "Absurd," he said. "What is life without passion?" He stared at her toe cleavage. "You have gorgeous feet, Professor Van Diemen."

"Why thank you, Dean Fortis." She gently pushed him away. He resisted for a moment until he realized what she intended to do. He removed her sandal. She lowered her foot onto his erection. He grabbed her ass again and pulled himself into her.

"Edmundo Castillo sandals?" he asked, his voice straining. She gently pushed on his cock. He groaned and pulled her back toward him.

"Yes. They were on sale at Bergdorf's." She pushed again. He pulled.

"I bought a pair of Manolo Blahnik crocodile boots when I was at a conference in San Antonio." Push. Pull.

"They are a lifetime investment," Van said in approval. Push. Pull. Push. Pull.

The dean tensed. His mouth opened, but no sound came out. Push. Pull. Push. Pull. Push. Pull. "Yes!" He released his grip and stepped away from her.

"Your timing is perfect," she smiled.

"What do you mean?"

"Your brother-in-law...." She motioned to Skip waving at them from the men's room door. "Carl Jung argued that from a single human's unconsciousness could be constructed all of human history."

The dean shook his head. "Jung never met Skip. Skip has the character of a root."

"No. I think Skip knows what he wants." Van lifted the beer to her lips. "But he won't take the risks necessary to get it."

The dean raised his pint and drank with her until both glasses were empty. "I am not like Skip in that regard." He motioned to Jeremiah to bring Van another. "You going to be here for a while? My suppers with Skip are mercifully brief." He put two $20 bills on the bar.

"I'll make myself comfortable." Van adjusted her tiny skirt as the dean put her sandal back on.

"And don't worry too much about the Religion Department." He ran his hand down her leg, and then reluctantly retreated from the bar to join Skip at a booth in the café section.

Jeremiah arrived moments later. "I'm surprised the dean left so quickly."

"He finished sooner than I'd hoped." Van smiled at the handsome bartender. He was not amused by her little joke. "We made plans to discuss my pre-tenure hearing later this evening."

"That's unfortunate." Jeremiah said softly as set down a mug of fresh-brewed coffee in front of her.

"And why is that?"

"Because I've arranged to get off early tonight."

Van tried to read his expression as he stood facing her. Jeremiah had obviously seen what she and the dean had done. She blushed and blew on the hot coffee to hide her discomfort. She didn't usually feel embarrassed about sex, even sex in public. She changed the subject. "Your beers are brilliant, you know."

"Is that why you pour so much of it down your throat?"

"Don't preach, Jeremiah."

He reached across the bar and gently touched her face. "I worry about you."

She set the coffee mug down and leaned into his hand. "Would you worry less if I dressed like Elizabeth Warren?"

"Dress any way that suits you." He stroked her curly brown hair. He glanced down the bar to the twins waving an empty margarita pitcher in his direction. "But if the dean gets tied up, I get off work at nine."

"Should I reserve the ladies room for then?" she joked lamely.

"No. I was thinking more in terms of my new four-poster bed." He seemed very serious. She visualized herself stripped down to her satin panties, while Jeremiah loomed above her.

"Sex on a bed? How quaint." Van stood up and adjusted her skirt above the tops of her nylons. "But right now, I've got to pee." She glanced up and saw that Jeremiah was staring, not at her legs, but into her eyes. "What's that look about?"

"I wasn't proposing we have sex." That took her back. "I'd like to make love. To you. Repeatedly. Exclusively." When she said nothing, Jeremiah noticed she was shifting from foot to foot. She really did have to pee. "Don't forget I get off at nine."

Van sighed. "I'm not very damned likely to forget, after what you just said." She wanted to stay and kiss him, but she'd already begun to leak.

When she returned from the ladies room, a man in charcoal Ralph Lauren suit and $200 silk tie was sitting next to her coffee. He was in his forties. He stared at Van as she eased onto her stool. Jeremiah had topped off the mug. The businessman straightened his tie. He reached for his wallet and checked its contents. When Jeremiah set a pint of porter in front of him, the man slid several bills in his direction. "Keep the change." The businessman took a sip of the porter and smiled. He leaned toward Van. "You on duty, darling?"

"Back off dickhead before I shove that pint glass up your ass."

The gentleman picked up his drink and moved down three stools next to the twins.

As Van raised the fresh coffee to her lips, she invoked the words of Porphyry, the third-century pagan philosopher: *Don't think of me as some person who can be recognized by the senses. My real self is distant from my body, colorless, shapeless, untouchable by human hands.* She imagined Jeremiah, naked, entering her, and never withdrawing. The dean and his promise of tenure she'd save for another day.

THE BAKERY BOY
Alegra Verde

I live in southwest Detroit on the tourist end of Mexican Town where the street is lined with beans and rice restaurants, and where dusty ponchos, sombreros, and maracas hang in shop windows. On weekends, chatty Canadians and adventurous suburbanites fill the restaurants' wrought-iron verandas, wagon wheel tables and booths. Mariachi and Tejano music spill out every time a customer opens a door. It's not a bad place to live; the Canadians are pretty tame and there's a park at the end of the block. The tiny square of park is mostly cement and steel spirals that really don't go with the 1930s brick and brass buildings, but I kinda like the way the old and the new clash. Just before the park is Panadería La Gloria. It's the best thing about living here cause I have a serious sweet tooth and the boy that works there is cute.

I'm a big girl, not fat, but I'm nearly six feet and a hundred and seventy five pounds, mostly muscle. I have to work out because I don't want to be somebody's bitch. I mean, the Latin Counts are tough on everybody, especially each other, but I don't like the way they treat their women, like meat, like a woman's only reason for existing is to serve and comfort the man that chooses her. That shit's not for me. I don't want to be somebody's mattress, a sperm repository, a milk cow for somebody's babies.

So, I don't fool with any of the guys on that level. I do my share on the street, collection mostly; I like numbers and have a good memory, and protection, sometimes, when it's needed. As long as the guys know they can rely on me and I don't fuck any of them, they leave me alone.

I know most of the Counts from high school. Most of them went to Western at one time or another, but I let it be known from the beginning that I wasn't looking for a man. A couple of them had to try me anyway, pressing their half-hard *vergas* up against my ass when they passed me from behind, or trying to feel up my *chichis*. So I had to remind them that I don't take no shit and I don't fight fair. I had to leave a couple of them with scars before they left me alone. Gordo was the most persistent. After that *pinche guey* had to get thirty-two stitches in his gut, he started calling me *una marimacha*. Some of the guys egged him on, trying to stir up more shit, but I just laughed it off. Everybody knows he's just an asshole! And I know I ain't no *tortillera*—I like men.

The guy who works at the bakery is almost as tall as me. He's not skinny, but he's kind of lanky. He has nice shoulders and arms like he works hard, but not like he's been lifting weights or hanging out at Gold's. Kind of shy, he never looks me directly in the eyes. When he gives me my change, it's sort of like he's staring at my *chichis*. But I don't feel like I need to bitch slap him or nothing because he's not trying to be an ass. He just don't have any social skills.

One night it was really late, I think it was a Thursday. I was watching Project Runway on Demand and I needed me a lemon *empanada* with my coffee. So I slid my feet into my flip-flops and pulled a shirt on over my bra and jean shorts. It was hot and we don't have air, so I usually strip down to a pair of shorts and a bra when I'm watching TV. I got a nice set of tits, a plush D, and I don't like them flopping around. Besides I don't want them to get like my mama's. She walks around in those snap front cotton robes and nothing else. *Ella tiene mangos bajitos.* So I keep on the bra for support rather than sitting around in just a t-shirt. I know, TMI. Anyway, I figured I'd dart around to La Gloria and pick up something to soothe my sugar Jones, an empanada, maybe a couple of ginger pigs and peek at the bakery boy.

He was inside sweeping. I could see him through the glass door. It was locked. I knocked on the glass and pointed to the knob. He looked up. He has really kind eyes. Big and brown, not weepy, but not happy either, more concerned. He unlocked the door and stood back a little before he said, "We're closed."

"I just wanted something sweet," I said slipping in and closing the door behind me. "I'll be quick."

"There's not much left." His smile was an apology.

"Any fruit *empanadas* or *carnitas* left?" I asked.

"No, but there's a few *ojos*."

They taste like dusty pound cake in an even dustier circle of crust sprinkled with sugar. Shaking my head, I frowned and asked, "Anything else?"

When he smiled at my grimace, his whole face brightened and he got even more handsome.

"We got some macaroons," he said watching my face for approval.

"I could do some coconut," I returned his smile and nodded.

He turned, took a couple of waxed sheets from the box on the shelf and headed over to the clear plastic fronted shelves that housed the baked goods.

I watched him. I liked the way his jeans hung just so, dipping low on his waist so I could see the tops of his boxers. I liked the way the fabric tightened over his *nalgas* when he bent over and the way his upper arm flexed, skin and muscle tightening as he reached deep into the bin. He ducked his head as he dipped further into the bin, a lock of straight black hair fell over one eye. His hair in back was tapered and razored clean at his neck.

"How many do you want?"

His voice sounded as though it came from a distance.

"How many you got?" I asked forgetting what we'd been talking about.

He shrugged, "About a dozen."

I laughed. "Two is good."

He turned back to me with two of the large macaroons wrapped loosely in paper.

"Here," he said handing them to me.

I dug into the pocket of my jean shorts for the money.

"That's OK," he said, grinning. "You're a regular. It's on the house."

I couldn't resist the grin. It was too much to ask. And I was horny, had been since I first set eyes on the bakery boy.

I wasn't a virgin. There'd been one guy before. He was a white guy. I figured he was safe because he wasn't one of us. I was seventeen. He told me he wasn't usually attracted to big girls, but that there was something sexy about me. He liked the way I moved. I was flattered and I was curious.

We did it during fifth hour under the retractable bleachers in the gym. The floor was hard and cold on my ass and he was in and out before the tardy bell rang. I knew there had to be more—I'd seen movies. But I figured it would take tests and trials like in chemistry class and I didn't want to get a rep as *una pisona*. But that was nearly two years ago and I was ready to try it again.

I took the macaroons from the bakery boy, set them down on the nearest table, and moved towards him. He backed up until he was flush against the plastic doors of the pastry bins. When he couldn't move any further, I pressed myself against him and watched as his eyes grew big and round. Then I pushed my *chichis* into his chest. I could feel the nipples getting hard and my *tetas* felt fuller, heavier. I wanted to lift and massage them to relieve the pressure, but instead I pressed then into his chest until the tips burrowed through the thin cotton of his t-shirt. His breathed hitched. His arms were stiff at his sides and his hands were splayed, fingers wide against the hard plastic doors of the pastry bins.

I reached down, unbuttoned his pants and slid my hand down into his shorts to gauge and stroke his *penga*. It was hot, slick, and long; I squeezed. His breath hitched. I pressed my nose into the crook of his neck. He smelled like cinnamon and sugar. I licked the sweet, hot flesh of his neck. He choked; a kind of cough followed by the screechy sound of his fingers as they slid across the hard plastic doors of the bins. The noise was like a surprise that punctuated the rustling sound of his breathing. His *penga* stretched and preened in my fingers.

"You got any condoms?" I asked.

He shook his head.

"When was the last time you were with a girl?"

He shook his head, left to right again and again until I pressed my lips to his. They were large and firm and warm. He opened welcoming my tongue, his tongue was timid at first, but quickly became eager sliding against mine. His mouth tasted like fresh bread. I nibbled a while enjoying the sweet savory taste of his tongue, his lips, and the warmth of his breath.

"Do you go with guys?" I asked pulling back a little so that I could see his response. He looked hurt; a furrow grew between his brows. He shook his head.

I kissed him again. He opened his mouth like he wanted more, so I rewarded him with a nip to his bottom lip, a quick pinch. He groaned and panted for more.

"Next time you'll have to bring a condom," I said unzipping his pants. He nodded and his hand found my ass, his fingers unsure.

"Unhook my bra," I said, between sucking his lip and dipping into the heat of his mouth.

His hands slid up under my shirt slowly as though marveling at the heat and smoothness of my skin. It was like being worshipped, so I let him take his time.

Pretty soon, he had the clasp undone and his fingers were finding their way to my breasts, playing over the skin until they discovered the stiff tips. He stopped as though surprised, and then his hot fingers probed and pulled at them, as though curious. The tugging was making me wet and I squirmed closer to him, but I let him continue to explore. Then he was rubbing the sensitive tip with the center of his palms rolling them in a circular motion.

By then my hands were pressed restlessly to the shelves on either side of his head. He was only a few inches shorter than me, but I stepped back so that he could put his hot mouth on my stiff, aching nipples. As he laved and sucked and tugged, the muscles deep inside my vagina clenched and more wetness seeped into my panties. The short spiky hairs at his nape pricked my fingers in a good way as I dragged them through the thick bristles and up through the lush longer locks. His mouth found the other nipple and tugged. My muscles answered. He groaned; the sound vibrated against my chest.

I stepped back, pushing him away, the nipple made a popping sound as it broke free of his eager mouth.

"Is there anyone else here?"

"No," he said, his eyes on my *chichis*.

"Lock the door and turn off the light," I said not wanting to offer a peep show to passersby.

He did as he was told.

The room was dark, lit only by the streetlights and the neon signs that advertised the stores across the street. The faint sweet smells of dough, cinnamon, and coconut seemed to grow stronger with the darkness.

He stood in front of me, waiting.

"Take off your pants."

He unzipped his pants the rest of the way and pushed them down along with his shorts, letting them slide down his legs before kicking them off and to the side. I wanted to giggle. He was standing in front of me bare assed with just a plain white t-shirt, white sport socks and a pair of Adidas.

"The shirt and socks, too."

In that light, he was beautiful, his skin pale, almost iridescent, the shadows highlighting the taut muscles of his stomach, the trim slope of his waist and the tension in his arms as he held them at his sides. His fingers twitched. I smiled. My fingers itched to touch him too. I wanted to run my fingers over the slight curve at his side, to trail along that sketchy indented swatch of skin that tapered down from his chest to his belly, to tangle my fingers in the shock of dark hair that surrounded the proud jut of his *penga*. He made me feel beautiful, the way he looked at me, the yearning in his eyes, the way his jaw trembled when he swallowed.

"Lay down over there," I pointed to the aisle between the pastry shelves where he had been sucking my breast.

I waited as he made a pallet of sorts out of his clothes. When he had stretched out on the lumpy pallet and propped himself up on his elbows, I kicked off my flip-flops. As he watched, I slid out of my shorts and then my panties. All the while, his *chorizo* was standing at attention.

I slipped my bra off through the armholes of my shirt and tossed it aside. I wasn't ready for the full-on naked thing yet—I was still a little self-conscious about my body. But I wanted to feel him chest-to-chest, pelvis-to-pelvis, so I unbuttoned my shirt.

"Lay back," I commanded as I stood over him. He did. I let him lay there a minute before I straddled him, lowered myself so that the wetness of my sex smashed and smeared against his belly and his thick, hot sausage butted against the crack of my ass.

Sitting up, he reached for me, his hands sliding over my hips, his open mouth sucking at the fleshy sides of my breasts. And then he was trying to flip me on to my back.

"No," I said pressing him back down. He fell back, barely containing his frustration. I pressed backwards, squeezing his *penga* between the cheeks of my ass. He held his breath, waiting. His hot hands pressed into my thighs, his fingers damp.

Good boy, I wanted to say, but I didn't. I liked that he controlled himself, that he could sense my limits and that he understood what I needed. I leaned forward, letting the hard tips of my breast drag up his stomach, his chest. He opened his mouth, ready, but I leaned in and gave him my tongue, my lips. He took them gratefully, his hand beneath my shirt stroking my back, my bottom, my thighs, stroking and squeezing, slow and rhythmic. My sex tightened, the juices flowing freely.

I pulled up onto my knees. He watched me, his hands stroking my thighs, as I maneuvered so that my sex was hovering just over his. Then I lowered myself onto him letting the knob, *la popeta*, push its way in, slow. Before he could thrust upwards, I lifted my bottom up until he slid all the way out before slowly pressing down again. I liked the way it felt when he entered me, liked the way the rounded head nudged its way in, spreading me, determined. So, I did it again, let him slip all the way out before pressing down again. He squeezed my thighs and thrust upwards. I held still. There was only so far he could go since he was flat on his back, I'd anchored my hands so that my palms pressed on his shoulders. He thrust up again and groaned in frustration, his blunt fingers scoring my thighs. He stared up at me, his eyes pleading. I slid down another inch. His eyes closed and I slid down, down, down until he filled me completely, his *penga* stretching and growing even harder as my heat surrounded him.

His hips bumped up and down like an egg boiling in a pot, as his fingers stroked my thighs and grabbed at my hips. I let him go for it, and then he was throbbing inside of me and I couldn't stay still. I lifted up, loving the slow drag of his flesh against my walls, the rasping heat as it rubbed and scratched at the itch deep inside of me. But then, I needed more so I pressed and pulled, down and up, the pace increasing as the friction flared setting fire to my senses. Each time I pressed and pulled, it seemed as though I was taking him deeper. Drawing him up, up, up until the knob was wedged just there, just there bobbing trying to touch, to reach something, but not quite. So, I lifted myself up until he hovered just at my opening before I took him in again, relishing the drag and pull of heated flesh against heated flesh as he thrashed beneath. My juices flowed freely into the prickly tufts at his groin, making scalding paths.

"Oh fuck, Mina," he shouted. I didn't even know he knew my name.

Sweat was trickling into my eyes and I couldn't see anymore. My fingers were slipping and sliding across his chest. He bucked beneath me, his back arching and ass rising in a feverish rhythm as he thrust upwards, rasping deep, deeper, touching and scoring me, just there, there, there and I was coming. A ripple and then a wave of something like electricity started tingling in my toes and twitching at my sex causing me to flex and tighten around him. The wave dragged me under sending a current through my body. He cried out and I could feel him pumping himself into me. His arms wrapped around my waist, his hands gripping my ass.

He must have been sitting up cause I could feel his slippery chest flush against mine, my breasts and sex smashed into him. We were roiling against the sea in an electric storm, the sweat like rain washing over us, the current rushing through me, purging my body of its need, soothing the itch until a cooling warmth surrounded me and all I could do was grin.

He had pulled me down so that I lay on top of him or maybe I had fallen, but he didn't seem to mind. After a minute or so, I got up anyway. I knew I must be heavy and I figured it was only polite. He looked startled when I moved away, probably because of what felt like an icy breeze that doused our sweat drenched bodies when we were no longer pressed together.

"Mina," he said, and then stopped like he was afraid to speak.

"This is just between me and you," I said as I stood and went about retrieving my clothes. "I don't want to hear about this from anybody else."

He nodded as he shrugged into his t-shirt.

I slipped into my panties and then my shorts. I found my bra and tucked it into my pocket, I'd put it back on when I got home. I needed to leave.

He pulled on his jeans and followed me to the door. "Mina." It sounded like a question. I unlocked the door. When I looked back at him over my shoulder, he was looking directly at me, at my face, not my *chichis*. He held his hand out to me. In it were the two macaroons wrapped in their waxed paper.

ETCHINGS
Cherry Wild

Laura goes into the bar and orders a drink. The last few weeks have been long and overflowing with work demands. She shrugs off her coat in an exaggerated fashion, in a way she knows emphasizes her curves and invites attention.

She perches on a seat at the bar, looking around to assess the men she's caught the attention of. Several are immediately dismissed. Too old. Too portly. Too pretty. Something not quite right in the eyes of the blond. Way too young. A woman with short dark hair catches her eye. Laura enjoys women, but thinks they are too difficult for casual sex.

The bartender brings Laura a vodka and tonic, and she purses her lips and sips.

A man with dark, curly hair that falls over his ears catches her eye. He is good looking and exudes confidence. Laura knows she also looks good, in her black pencil skirt and silky purple blouse, and she also feels confident.

She smiles and nods her head to ask "Join me?" He smiles his agreement and Laura returns his smile.

"Hello there," he says. He slides onto the seat next to her, intentionally brushing her legs as he does so.

Laura smiles at him, running her finger along the rim of her glass.

Over their first two drinks, they exchange pleasantries and share brief details about work—establishing that neither is questionable, nor undesirable. They lightly touch each other in passing, a hand on the arm here, a hand on the knee there.

Over their third drink, they talk movies. She turns to face him full on, and threads her foot between his legs, resting the ball of her foot on the low rung of his bar stool. She rocks her knee back and forth, causing Paul to lose his words. He caresses the back of her knee and Laura makes a humming sound in approval.

As they finish their third drinks, Paul says. "So—"

"Yes?" Laura says.

"Would you like to go someplace more…not here?"

Laura smiles slowly, tilting her head to the side. "And what would we do 'not here'?"

"I could," Paul chuckles, "show you my etchings."

Paul has pressed her knee between his legs. She laughs and uses both hands to push his knees apart, and then stands up directly in front of him. Leaning forward slightly, so that her breasts fall lightly against his chest, she brushes a curl away from his left ear and whispers "yes."

Laura collects her things and saunters towards the front of the bar, waiting for Paul to join her.

"Do you live far?" She asks, slipping her arm into his. He presses her arm close to him, tightly.

"No, actually." Paul says, his voice husky and low.

"Good." Laura says.

"I bet you are a handful," Paul says.

Laura smiles wryly in response, but says nothing.

Paul leads her to an older brick building. It is well tended and solid, attractive.

"Follow me," Paul says, opening and holding the door open for her.

"With pleasure," Laura responds.

"We are going to have an amazing time," Paul says, a smile dancing on his lips.

As soon as they are in his apartment, they are making out before their coats can hit the floor. He starts walking her down a long hallway.

"I suppose I should be a gentleman. Offer you a drink." Paul says, pulling away from Laura.

She is breathless, her cheeks and chest aflame. It was cold outside and it is warm inside Paul's apartment.

"Would you like something to drink?" Paul asks, with a mock formality, a laugh twitching at his lips.

Laura looks at him, taking him in. He really is gorgeous. An almost-athletic build and he is a close to six-feet tall. She steps forward and puts her hands on his biceps. His muscles tense under the lightweight sweater he is wearing and she caresses his arms.

"I'd prefer it if you weren't a gentleman," Laura says. Her voice is heavy and she can feel how damp her panties are. When she presses herself against him, his erection twitches against her hip.

He lowers his mouth to hers and kisses her deeply, running his fingers through her hair and holding it tightly. He lightly tugs her hair and a guttural sound escapes her mouth.

She pulls away momentarily, panting.

"Just a couple of things, first," Laura says, catching her breath.

"Yes?" Paul asks. Laura can see a look of apprehension flicker across his eyes.

"If want to do anything particularly kinky, please ask me first," Laura asks.

"Of course," Paul says, looking perplexed. "Why would I not do that as a matter of course?"

"I do not mean this as an accusation or comment about you personally," Laura says, feeling a moment of fluster. "I had a difficult experience not so long ago. It was…unpleasant."

"I am sorry to hear that." Paul says, reassuringly. "I can assure you that my tastes are reasonably pedestrian. Unless there is something in particular that you like?"

"Well," Laura says, "I am open to kinky, but it's not what I'm after tonight, honestly."

"What do you want to avoid?"

"Anal sex. Just, not my thing. Whether it is with a toy or not."

"Again that's not a problem." Paul says, "I have some kinks, but I don't go in for that either."

"OK," Laura says, feeling relief as Paul says this. In Laura's experience, casual sex can be a minefield. As confident as she feels about sex, there is always that moment of 'will we be compatible?' when sleeping with someone for the first time.

"Are there any other boundaries I should know about?" Paul asks.

"Not off the top of my head." Laura says.

"I understand," Paul says warmly. "Do you feel comfortable?"

"I do, thanks." Laura says.

For the first time, Laura takes her eyes off Paul and looks around the room. It looks like a fairly masculine home. A brown leather couch, a big flat screen TV, several bookshelves filled to overflowing with hardcover and paperback books. There is some art on the walls, but there is not enough light for her to see them clearly, though the colors seem dark and abstract. She likes what she sees, both in the apartment and the man in front of her.

"Well then," Paul says, grabbing the lapels of her coat and pulling her close to him, "let's see what kind of pleasure we can find."

"Yes, please," Laura says. She surrenders to his kiss and wraps her arms tightly around his torso, sliding her hands towards the waistband of his jeans.

While kissing her deeply, Paul runs his hands up and down her back, then over her shoulders and down the front of her blouse. Laura feels her nipples harden as he runs his hands down the sides of her breasts, though he carefully avoids touching them, even when she tilts her body to his hands, like a flower reaching towards the sun. His hands continue down her stomach and to the top of her thighs, and again he avoids touching the area of her sex. She pushes her body closer to him, yet he holds her back a little.

"Don't rush," Paul says. He takes his time unbuttoning her blouse, before laying it across a chair. Then, he spends several minutes running his hands a few millimeters above her skin. Occasionally he leans in and breathes heavily against her; her neck, the curve of her waist, the back of her knee. She finds this deeply erotic and the hair on her arms is alert to Paul's every movement. She starts to push forward, but he steps back and smiles.

"Slowly," he says. He takes another step back, before starting to unbutton his shirt. He places his shirt over hers on the chair. "Now, your turn. And remember, no touching."

Laura smiles and moves over to him. She holds up her hands and starts at his wrist, then moves her hands up his arms. His arms are not particularly hairy and there is only a shock of hair on his chest. His skin is a Mediterranean olive color; unblemished and incredibly smooth.

As Laura runs her hands just above his skin, moving from his arms to his shoulder to his chest, where she lingers, she can see goose bumps on his skin, trailing after where her hands have been, despite the warmth of the apartment and the heat between them. Paul's eyes are at half mast and he has a smile on his face. He looks faintly drugged.

"Do you see?" He asks. His voice has a guttural quality to it.

"I do. I like this," Laura admits. The mix of slowness and anticipation and not-touching is heady and seductive.

"Well, let us see what other pleasures we can discover together," Paul gasps as her hand moves across his stomach and towards his hip.

"Oh, yes please," Laura says, smiling so broadly her cheeks feel strained.

"Take off your pants," Laura asks.

"If you demand," Paul replies, a twinkle in his eye. He arches one of his eyebrows.

"I do demand. I want to see what I have to look forward to." Laura says, stepping back and asserting control. "Strip."

"Yes, ma'am!" Paul says quickly, smiling his approval. There is an admiration and relief she sees in his eyes, one that she has seen with other men who appreciate a woman who exerts some control during sex.

Paul takes his time removing the belt from his jeans, sliding it out of the belt loops and wrapping it around his palm. He removes the belt from his hand, before moving towards a window that has the curtains open. A shaft of light comes in from a street light. All this time, they have been moving around in the near dark, illuminated only by ambient light. The shaft of light illuminates him more clearly. As he unzips and slips off his jeans, Laura catches her breath. She has always been a sucker for a man with good legs and Paul has the legs of a soccer player.

He starts to walk over to her, but Laura holds up her hand and says, "No. Wait."

Paul smiles in response and returns to the window.

Laura smiles. She unzips her skirt and shimmies out of it, turning around as she does so. She hears a sharp intake of breath from Paul, as she spreads her legs and bends over. Then, she turns around and stands in front of him, wearing nothing but her bra, panties, and sheer black pantyhose, and her heels.

"Shall I continue?" She asks sultrily, cupping her lace-covered breasts.

"No," Paul says, a hitch in his voice. "Please, come over to the couch and sit down."

"Yes, sir," she says, then casually makes her way to the couch. She sits on the edge, but he comes over and pushes her so she sits further back. He kneels before her and spreads her legs. He gently lifts her feet, slips her shoes off, and gently massages the arches of her feet. Laura groans lightly in pleasure. Heels make her legs look spectacular, but wearing them exacts a knotty price.

"You like that?" He asks.

"Most definitely," Laura responds, her mouth curling into a wide smile.

"Now scoot forward," Paul commands. He scoots closer to the edge of the couch, on his knees.

"If you demand," Laura says.

"I do demand," Paul echoes.

She scoots forward to the edge of the couch, her legs splayed on either side of Paul. Quickly reaching up to her hips, Paul grabs the waistband of her pantyhose and panties and starts pulling them down. In response, Laura lifts her hips.

"Yesss," Paul says. His voice is thick with desire.

Laura's body is bursting with heat. Her sex pulses in response to his body.

Paul takes his time as he pulls her pantyhose down her legs, kissing her legs as skin is revealed, paying extra attention to the side of her knee. Laura gasps as she lowers her ass back on to the couch, its texture cool on her bare ass. The scent of her sex rises into the room as she spreads her legs before him.

Paul runs his hands along the length of Laura's legs—touching her softly, but definitely touching her. Laura's sexual frustration starts to unfurl and change tempo. She leans back, closes her eyes, and moans slightly. She sinks into the pleasure of the moment and savors it.

After avoiding her sex for so long, Laura cries out in surprise when Paul runs the tip of a finger very close to her clit. She arches her back and he circles her clit.

"Oh, yes. Yes, very much." Laura moans as Paul lightly massages her clit.

Paul says nothing, but his touch becomes firmer and Laura gasps loudly. Then, Paul is kissing the inside of her thighs, patiently making his way up towards her sex. Paul places his mouth on her sex and firmly presses her clit with his tongue. She feels like she is going to burst in pleasure before much longer.

In quick succession, Paul puts two fingers inside her and rotates them slowly, while working his tongue over her clit more and more, with increasing firmness. Laura is crying out and moaning, grinding her hips against his mouth. She can feel his whiskers tickle against the inside of her thighs as they vibrate in pleasure.

Laura feels a thick and warm tension radiating from her center. It won't be much longer before her nerve endings burst like an exploding star.

Sensing her orgasm, Paul starts to speed up his fingers, and sucks more and more loudly and firmly. Laura's insides tighten in a hot mass and a bright white light of pleasure explodes in her. Her body clenches and expands and contracts, out of her control. She pushes her hips towards Paul's mouth—she wants him to devour her. It has been a long time since anyone eat her out with such precision before.

Laura throws her head back and a sound like a whimper and a moan escapes her mouth. Paul pulls her closer to him and sucks even harder.

"Oh yes! Just...that!" She screams, crumpling into a weak mess. She reaches out with her hands to try and grab onto something. Her body spasms as she comes hard. Paul starts kissing the inside of her thighs again.

"That was perfect," Laura finally says. "I..."

"Don't speak," Paul says, rising his head for a moment, "just enjoy."

Paul finishes his attentions and remains sitting in front of her, his hands caressing the length of her legs.

"So, if I am correct, I would like to believe that you enjoyed yourself there."

Laura laughs throatily. "You might say that was an accurate description of the situation."

"Now," Laura continues, leaning forward and running her hands through his hair, "what can I do to make you feel the same way?"

"Are you ready for more?" Paul asks playfully.

"In a moment, yes," Laura says, looking Paul directly in the eyes.

"Should we stay here? Or go into the bedroom?" Laura asks, lightly touching the side of Paul's jaw. He leans into her touch, all the while maintaining eye contact with Laura.

"I would like you suck me, but only a little." Paul says.

"Then please, let us switch positions," Laura says, standing up.

Paul stands up and kisses Laura on the mouth. At first, Laura is surprised. She has had men and women eat her out before, but few of them have ever kissed her immediately afterwards. She enjoys it and she kisses him back with renewed fervor.

"Hm, I see," Paul says.

"What?" Laura asks, confused.

"Oh, nothing," Paul evades her question. He switches positions with her and sits down on the edge of the couch.

"Allow me," Laura says, kneeling down before Paul.

Laura lightly runs her hands up and down Paul's legs, similar to the way he did with her. Then she reaches up and pushes him back, so that he is leaning fully back against the couch. And instead of taking her time, she lightly holds his penis and then slips the full length into her mouth.

Paul moans in surprise and pleasure, and moves his hips. Within seconds, he is rock hard and Laura is pleased at his response to her. She slows down her sucking, and runs her tongue up and down the length of his hard cock. He shudders and runs his hand through her hair.

"No touching, remember?" She demands.

Paul groans and moves his hand.

Laura teases the tip of his cock, lightly licking and sucking it, running her tongue around its head. When she feels Paul twitching under her tongue, she opens her mouth wide and plunges her mouth and tongue down the length of him. Paul calls out her name and pushes up against her. Putting her hands on his hips, she pushes him down and holds him down.

"Don't stop!" Paul says, almost pleading, as she stands up.

Laura looks at him and smiles. Paul's eyes are dilated and his cheeks and chest are flushed.

"You said 'only a little'…." she teases. She reaches over to her purse and removes a condom.

She kneels before Paul and unrolls the condom over his cock. He twitches when she's finished and she kisses him where his shaft meets his groin.

Laura pushes his knees together and climbs on his lap. Paul smiles as if drugged and happy.

Reaching down, she grabs his cock and then slides herself over his cock. Teasing him, she raises and lowers herself over just the tip of his cock, never letting him slide out. When she can't take the anticipation any more, she lets herself drop down the full length of his cock.

"Oh, wow," Laura gasps. His cock is a perfect length—it has the right amount of thickness and isn't show-off big. She raises and lowers herself again, before resuming rocking back and forth.

"Oh god, Laura…that feels amazing." Paul says, throwing back his head. His eyes are unfocused and his eyelids are drooping.

Laura slips off her bra and lifts one of her breasts up to his mouth. Greedily, Paul sucks her nipple hard, lightly nipping at it and roughly flicking it with his tongue.

"Yes!" Laura cries out.

Without warning, Laura slows down. She teases the tip of his cock, again, riding the head. When Paul starts panting harder, Laura drops down fully and grinds down as far as she can go.

"Oh fuck, that's perfect," Paul exclaims. He reaches down and grabs a hold of her hips, and times his thrusts to counterpoint her rocking.

Their breathing quickens and their skin glistens with rivulets of sweat. A primal, musky scent fills the air.

Laura grabs Paul's shoulders and starts rocking back and forth and raising and lowering herself along the full length of his cock, while Paul squirms below her and thrusts up into her. She lowers her mouth onto his and kisses him deeply. She can feel another orgasm building quickly. His cock is perfectly rubbing against her g-spot with every stroke.

"YES!" Laura calls out, her second orgasm catching her by surprise, her body shuddering in a fresh wave of spasms. She sees Paul watching her and it's clear that her pleasure is sending him over the edge, too. Paul bucks beneath her as her second orgasm spasms through her. He wraps his arms around her torso tightly, pulling her tightly against his chest, before throwing back his head.

"AAHHH!" Paul cries out, not breaking his hold on her.

They both slow their movements, but still rock together lightly, riding out their orgasms together.

They are both quiet for a couple of minutes, catching their breath and refocusing their eyes. Laura leverages her sweat-slicked body up and off of Paul.

"That was amazing," Paul says, reaching out and putting a hand on Laura's leg.

"Yeah, it was. Thank you," Laura says, putting her hand on his.

"If that offer for a drink still stands, some water or juice would be wonderful," Laura says.

"Of course."

While Paul is gone in the kitchen, Laura stretches and luxuriates in how good her body feels in this moment. Her body is humming with pleasure and the tightness in her shoulders is gone.

"Here you are," Paul says, handing her a glass of orange juice.

Laura drinks the juice in two gulps.

They recline against the couch, bodies touching. Paul's arm is around Laura's shoulders, and he lightly strokes her arm as they idly chat about music, but they don't find an easy common thread like they did earlier. From the sound of it, Paul listens to a lot of indie or local bands, and Laura has always preferred classic rock or classical.

"What time is it?" Laura asks.

Paul twists around and looks at a clock. "About midnight."

"I should get going, then," Laura says, leaning over to kiss him before she stands up.

"Mmm," Paul says, rubbing one hand on her arm and tickling her knee with the other. "You don't have to go."

"I have an early meeting," Laura lies. It is a small lie, but all she wants now is to go home and sleep in her own bed...alone.

Laura dresses quickly and picks up her purse.

"Do you need me to call you a taxi?" Paul asks. He pulls his boxers on and stands in front of her, partially lit by the ambient light coming through the window. In all of this, he never fully turned on the lights in his apartment.

"No. I'll be fine." Laura smiles.

"See you again sometime?" Paul asks.

"It's possible." Laura evades. She doesn't tell him that they are practically neighbors. While she doesn't plan to see him again, she figures it is inevitable that they will run into each other again, since Portland is a cozy city. She wonders what Paul would be like as a regular partner and suspects she would greatly enjoy that. Yet, she's not looking for a relationship, casual or otherwise. There is too much going on in her life, career-wise, for her to consider maintaining a relationship. Instead, she has found great satisfaction in treating herself to a man now and then, for an evening of fun.

Paul walks her to the door and they kiss again.

As Laura pulls away from the kiss, something catches her eye, causing her to laugh.

Paul follows her eyes.

"I wasn't joking when I said I had etchings," he says, a smile playing across his lips. "I bought these in Spain…three, four years ago."

Laura takes a hard, quick look at them. "Your etchings are exquisite," she says.

Still smiling, she gives him another lingering kiss, before turning and walking away, feeling sated and relaxed.

PARTY GIRL
Rachael Knight

I leaned against the kitchen counter and sipped my drink, the generous helping of vodka scratching at my throat. There was some soda in there too, but it was fighting a losing battle. This wasn't my first drink for the night or my second, if I was being honest, but I needed to take emergency action if I was going to get through this party.

It was 7pm. The guests would be arriving soon. I finished the rest of my drink in two large gulps and set the glass aside. Playing hostess always made me so nervous. Would everybody have a good time? Would the music I'd chosen be cool enough? The answer to both questions was "probably not." Parties were not worth the stress, which is why I never had them, or attended them, if I could help it. Somehow, Sarah had managed to talk me into this one. She'd said she couldn't imagine having her thirtieth anywhere else. I must have been temporarily insane when I agreed, or drunk.

The sound of the doorbell bounced through the apartment. *Shit.* A large part of me had been hoping nobody would show. I smoothed my dress down over my hips, picking off imaginary pieces of lint. Sarah had bought it for me, I guessed as compensation, and insisted I wear it tonight. It was emerald green, my favorite color, and the material clung to me like a second skin, showing off more curves than I was comfortable with. I made my way to the front door, taking small steps, tentative in my heels. The sound of voices and laughter from the hall pushed against the door, impatient. Savoring my last moment of peace, I pulled it open, letting the noise spill inside.

"Happy birthday to me!" Sarah squealed, jiggling up and down. She was surrounded by a large group of people, most of whom I didn't know.

They all looked in some way the same, a gaggle of hipsters with beards and rolled up jeans.

"You look fantastic in that dress. What did I tell you?" she said.

"Thanks Sarah, you look great too." Sarah always looked great. Even in high school when the rest of us were dealing with pimples and braces, Sarah seemed immune to all that teenage awkwardness. I however, had never managed to grow out of it, still feeling like I didn't fit inside my own body, even at twenty-eight.

"These are some of my friends from work," Sarah said. "I knew you wouldn't mind if I invited them along as well. Now, let's get fucked up!" She thrust a bottle of champagne into the air as if she were leading a charge to battle and strode into the hall. On her way past me she whispered into my ear, "Lose the underwear, girl. Nobody likes VPL."

Heat shot into my cheeks. Great, tonight was off to a bad start already. Sarah's posse followed her down the hallway, carrying bottles of tequila and cases of beer. It didn't look like I was going to make it to bed before sunrise.

"Just head into the lounge," I called after them. "I'll be there in a second." I ducked into my bedroom and looked in the mirror. Sarah was right, even the seamless panties I was wearing could be seen through the thin fabric of the dress.

They'd have to come off.

At least the alcohol in my bloodstream was making this an easier decision. I quickly slid off my underwear and tossed them aside. Much better. But now I was completely naked under my dress. The cut of the material already made it impossible to wear a bra. How could I go out there like this? I took a few deep breaths and told myself to get it together, to be brave. Tonight, I wouldn't care what anybody else thought.

The doorbell rang again and I went to answer it, dragging my fledgling courage behind me. The silky fabric of the dress brushed against my bare skin with every stride and brought a smile to my lips. It made me feel like I had a secret. It made me feel sexy. I pulled open the door, armed with a new resolve to have a good time tonight.

A man stood on the landing, holding a bunch of flowers. He was wearing a suit, impressive. It had obviously been tailored for him, too, hugging the contours of his broad shoulders. Maybe this was Sarah's latest plaything? He looked like her type: tall, muscular, with just the right amount of stubble shading his jaw. But I supposed a guy that good looking must be everybody's type.

"Is this Sarah's thirtieth?" he asked.

"Yep, come on in."

"Oh, great. I wasn't sure if I'd gotten the right place."

I held out my hand. "I'm Sarah's friend Emma. The idiot who agreed to host this party."

He placed his hand in mine, his grip firm and warm, and a liquid feeling washed through me, dissolving my bones one by one. A sensation that I couldn't entirely blame on the alcohol. I had the unexpected urge to slip my hand under the sleeve of his jacket and run my fingers across the fine, dark hairs on his wrist. He chuckled, and I realized that I was staring at him like a ravenous teen. I needed to get a hold of myself. The first man to show up at my house with flowers and I was weak at the knees. Still holding my hand in his, he said, "It's very nice to meet you Emma. I'm Sam."

"You, too." I smiled, ignoring the back flips my stomach was performing. My skin felt hyper-sensitive against my dress, and I was all too conscious of my lack of underwear. "Sarah's in the lounge if you want to head in," I said, looking away from him, pretending to scrutinize the peeling paint on the door frame. I expected him to let go of me and step inside, but he didn't, instead he kept looking at me, a half-smile on his lips.

"That is a beautiful dress," he said. He admired me openly, his gaze running over the contours of my body, making me feel like he could see straight through my clothing, as if I were standing naked in front of him. My body responded automatically, my nipples tightening at the thought. *Traitors.* I'd bet he looked at everyone like that, was used to women throwing themselves at him. Besides, there were much prettier girls inside to claim his attention.

"Thank you," I said, and extricated my hand from his grip. The smart thing to do would be to stay well clear of him. At least it would stop me from embarrassing myself any further.

I tried to ignore it, but something had shifted inside me, like a knot had loosened in my abdomen, allowing me to breathe. It had been so long since someone had looked at me that way. Since Steve had left me for someone blonder, sexier, I'd kept my desire locked inside me like a criminal. Now, it was threatening to escape.

*

By 10pm my apartment was choked with bodies. Sarah's friends filled every available space, leaning against the walls, perching on the arms of sofas, and sprawling over the floor. A haze of cigarette smoke hung heavy in the air, making everything appear soupy, dreamlike. If I closed my eyes and counted to ten would they all disappear? I gave it a go, squeezing my eyes shut and counting slowly. No such luck. When I opened them again, the bodies were still there; in fact, it even seemed like there were more of them.

My glass was empty. I navigated a path to the kitchen, avoiding outstretched arms and legs. The kitchen was quiet, the eye of the storm. The tornado of bodies had already ripped through, leaving heavy debris in its wake: plastic cups strewn across the counter and chips smashed into the floor. I sighed and leaned against the counter, savoring the peace for a moment.

"Enjoying the party?"

I spun around, startled. Sam stood behind me, a beer in each hand.

"I had to go bathtub diving for these two. Pickings are getting slim out there." He looked so proud, like the beers were wild animals that he had hunted and killed himself. He held one out towards me, the cap already removed.

"Thanks," I said, and took a sip, the cold liquid foaming over my tongue. He looked so at home in a stranger's kitchen, leaning against the bench and twirling a bottle opener in one hand. It made me feel self-conscious, as if I were the one who didn't belong.

"So what's your story?" I asked. "How do you know Sarah?"

"I don't really. We worked together a couple of years ago. I was pretty surprised to receive an invitation. I think she must have invited everyone she's ever met."

"I think you might be right."

The conversation gave way to silence and I searched for something to say, conscious of the heat spreading up my neck. He sipped his beer and watched me, the smile fading out of his eyes, replaced by something base, primal. I shivered, goose bumps prickling along my arms. Suddenly the room felt claustrophobic, like all the air had been sucked out of it. I needed to do something to distract myself.

"Do you want something stronger?" I asked. "I have some vodka stashed away."

"Sounds great."

I turned and reached up to the top cupboard for a glass, glad to do something to break the tension. My clothes felt uncomfortably tight. As I reached for the glass, my movement pulled the hem of my dress upwards, inching it up my thighs until the material was barely covering my naked buttocks. I knew Sam was watching me and I resisted the urge to tug down my dress, the alcohol making me bold. He was doing it again, making me feel like my clothing had vanished, making me feel sexy, something I hadn't felt in a long time. I gave in to the feeling, letting the knot inside me loosen further. Closing my eyes, I imagined myself naked, pressed against the bench, my legs spread for him. I didn't know anything about this man, but I didn't care. Tonight, I would take what I wanted.

He stepped up behind me, his body heat burning through my dress.

"You have no idea how sexy you are, do you?" he whispered in my ear. His arms circled me, trapping me against him, his erection hard against my back. A warm ache flared between my legs and spread throughout my groin, almost painful in its intensity. I gasped, shocked by the violence of my desire. For someone who had spent so long telling myself I didn't need this, it was far too easy to let my body take control. Sam's hands cupped my breasts and he flicked his thumbs across my nipples, sending bolts of lightning through my body. I arched into him, wanting his hands to be everywhere at once.

"I want to see you," he said.

Heat coursed through me and I nodded, unable to squeeze any words out of my clouded brain. He bent me over the counter and traced his fingers up my thighs, stopping when he reached the hem of my dress.

"You don't have anything on under this dress, do you?" Without waiting for an answer, he grabbed the fabric and pulled it upwards, exposing all of me. Groaning, he cupped my buttocks, teasing me with his fingers. I was swollen and wet, my body ready for him to push inside me right now.

"Please," I whimpered, pressing back against him.

"Spread your legs for me."

I did as I was told, spreading myself wide open.

"Now, stay right where you are," he said. "You're so beautiful like that."

He stepped backwards to look at me. I imagined what I would look like through his eyes, my body bent over, wet and ripe, moisture trickling from my center. If I had any reservations left about giving myself to this stranger, they fell away as he hovered his fingers over my sex.

"Do you want this?" he asked, grazing my sensitive skin, but holding back from giving me what I needed.

"Yes. Please." I was almost panting with desire.

Finally, he ran his fingers over my clitoris, then plunged them inside me. I let out a loud groan and pushed myself onto him, wanting his fingers deeper.

"Hey Sarah, grab me a drink," someone yelled from the lounge, the sound of their voice cascading into the kitchen like they'd thrown a bucket of iced water.

Oh no. We were in my kitchen, in the middle of a goddamn party. Anyone could walk in and see me like this. I pushed Sam off me and yanked my dress back into place. What had seemed erotic a minute ago, now seemed stupid and embarrassing. I couldn't believe how reckless I'd been. Sam didn't seem fazed. He winked at me and said, "We'll finish this in your bedroom. I'll meet you there in five," then disappeared back into the party before I could reply. I was still trying to collect myself when Sarah bounced around the corner, glassy eyed and swinging a half-drunk bottle of Moët back and forth.

"Hey there," she said when she spotted me. "What are you doing in here all alone?"

"I was just, um, getting someone a glass." I picked up the glass I had reached for earlier and held it out in front of me as proof. "See."

"Okay, well you should get out here. I have someone I want you to meet." She dragged me into the lounge and I didn't have the strength to resist. My body and mind were still throbbing from Sam's touch.

Re-joining the party was like entering an alien landscape. Rubbish and articles of clothing littered the carpet. My apartment looked like a frat house. Sarah deposited me next to a weedy man, whose shirt was at least two sizes too big for his small frame.

"This is Chris. He's an accountant. I think you guys will have a lot in common."

Her mission completed, Sarah swirled back into the whirling mass of bodies on the dance floor. I tried to focus my attention on the man in front of me. He looked uncomfortable, not quite sure where he should be standing or whom he should be talking to. Parties were not his natural habitat. Was this the kind of person Sarah thought I would be interested in, someone boring and meek? Is that what she thought I was?

"Nice to meet you Chris," I said, "but I have to go. Have a great night." I squeezed myself through the tunnel of people lining the hallway and slipped into my bedroom. My heart was thumping. The spicy scent of my cinnamon candle filled the air and I breathed it in, calming myself. In the quiet and dark I could almost believe there was no party at all. I paced the room, turning on lamps and straightening pillows. Maybe he wasn't coming? He could've met a more interesting girl. There were plenty to choose from. I sat down on my bed, which hadn't seen any action for way too long.

There was a soft knock at the door and my breath caught in my chest. What should I do now? Lean seductively in the bathroom doorway? Spread out naked on the bed like they did in the movies? The door opened before I could move. Sam shut it behind him and shrugged off his jacket, folding it over the back of a chair.

"I didn't know if you would be here," he said, unbuttoning his shirt and tossing it aside. "But I'm very glad you are."

My groin tightened at the sight of his bare chest. His skin was smooth and tan and I ached to touch him.

"Let's pick up where we left off then," he said, his eyes darkening. "Take off your dress."

The rapid rise and fall of my breasts gave away my uneven breathing as I undid the clasp around my neck and let my dress fall to the floor. His eyes devoured my body, lingering on my taut nipples. Before tonight I would've felt vulnerable, exposed, letting someone see me like this, but instead I felt powerful, unashamed of my desire. His erection strained against his trousers as I trailed my fingers across my breasts, reveling in my body's ability to arouse him. I teased my aching nipples with my fingers and squeezed, gasping at the delicious pain. Sam's breath rushed out of him in a hiss and he grabbed me, kissing me hard, our tongues clashing and stroking against each other. A pulse thrummed between my legs. Just his kiss had me ready. His hot mouth traced down my neck and over my breasts to where I wanted him most. He suckled hard at my nipples, circling and flicking the sensitive nubs with his tongue, chasing any thoughts out of my head, except for how good his mouth felt against my skin. I arched my neck and moaned, feeling my wetness slick on my thighs. He slipped his hand between my legs and thrust his fingers inside me, stroking my clit with his thumb, pushing me higher, bringing me closer to the edge. My cries escalating, I moved my hips back and forth, pushing myself against him, wanting release.

"Not yet," he said, and pulled his hand away, leaving my skin throbbing for more. "I'm going to take you to the edge again and again, and when you can't take it anymore I'll make you come so hard the whole party will hear you scream." He pushed me down onto the bed, spreading my legs and kneeling in front of me. Slowly he began lapping at my sex, his tongue gliding across me with long strokes, then flicking across my clit. He slid his fingers into me, thrusting them in and out until I was whimpering with pleasure. As I was about to tip over the edge, he stopped, waiting until my cries subsided. It was the sweetest kind of torture. My body craved release and I needed him inside me. My hips bucked, silently asking him to fuck me.

"What do you want Emma?"

I shuddered as he circled his tongue around my clit.

"Tell me what you want me to do to you," he repeated.

I hesitated. The words were stuck in my throat. I wanted to let go, but something was still holding me back. I'd never experienced someone so devoted to my pleasure, not asking anything in return, not expecting me to be someone I wasn't. Sam took off his trousers and kicked them aside, leaving him naked. I admired the hard length of him and knew he would fit perfectly inside me, filling me completely. He lent over me and bent my knees up against his chest. Slowly, he pushed his cock against my opening and I began to pant, begging him to possess me. He stopped, hovering, not letting more than the tip of himself enter me. Never had I wanted someone so badly. My whole body ached with need. He began to stoke my swollen clit, faster and harder. I cried out and pushed my hips forwards, desperate to feel him moving within me, but he pulled back again.

"What do you want Emma? Do you want me to fuck you?" He continued to stroke me and I writhed underneath him, my moans getting louder in time with the pressure building inside me. I nodded.

"Tell me."

The confidence I had locked away for so long broke loose, filling me with an amazing sense of freedom. I looked him right in the eyes and said, "I want you to fuck me, Sam, until I don't know who I am anymore."

He smiled and thrust himself into me, stretching me taut. I let out a guttural groan, feeling my muscles contracting around his length. Our bodies finally joined, he began to move, thrusting slowly at first and then faster, slamming in and out of me with long strokes, his moans mingling with mine. He plunged deeper and deeper inside me, making me his and setting my body on fire. Waves of sensation coursed through me and I let go. I came hard, throwing my head back and screaming my pleasure to the ceiling. Sam continued to thrust in and out of me, taking me further and higher until I wanted to beg him to stop. With one final thrust, Sam came with me, shuddering and groaning, releasing himself inside me.

I was floating above my body, watching us tangled in each other, our bodies softened by sex. As I drifted back into myself, I expected to feel awkward, like I have before when sharing that kind of intimacy with someone, but I didn't. I ran my hand over Sam's firm buttocks and smiled.

Maybe I could be a party girl after all.

ENEMY EXCHANGE
Lynn Lake

The war was finally over! We could all hardly believe it. After three long years, the Korean "conflict" was at last at an end.

I'd only been on the peninsula for six months, stationed at a mobile army surgical hospital located just south of the 38th parallel. Long enough to get my lifelong fill of combat casualties and a lifelong commitment to my future husband, Gordon.

Gordon was a doctor at the tent hospital, while I was a nurse. It had been love at first sight and now we planned on getting married when we returned stateside.

Gordon and I grinned at one another across the reveling throng in the mess tent. We wedged our way through the olive drab-clad crowd and met at the flimsy screen doors, took each other's hands and strolled out into the sunlight, leaving the base party behind.

It was a beautiful summer day, July 27th, the sun beaming down out of a bright blue sky. The camp, a collection of green canvas tents and corrugated steel supply sheds, was surprisingly quiet, almost everybody mobbing in the mess for the official celebration. There were just the occasional stray dog, and smiling and bowing South Koreans to greet us as we made our way down the dusty road that led out of the camp.

We walked for miles, walking on air, nothing to fear now after all of those seemingly endless days and nights of artillery barrages and sniper attacks, enjoying the rugged countryside that had once seemed so foreboding and that now seemed so picturesque in the afternoon sunlight.

Our perspectives had already changed, our moods so lightened after bearing the weight of war for so long. Gordon had been in Korea for nine months. He smiled at me like a little boy, tightly gripping my hand.

I smiled happily back at him, admiring, as always, his rugged, strong-jawed face and bright blue eyes, the red curls peeking out from under his green Army cap. He cut a fine figure in his uniform, his major's gold oak leaves glinting on his collar in the sun. I was dressed in my green khakis, as well, and as we wandered off the road and into the wooded wilderness, it seemed like a splendid idea to shed these military uniforms. Free ourselves from the trappings of war and to fully mark the peace.

Gordon had the same idea as me. We stopped in a grass clearing amongst the trees and turned to face each other. We didn't speak a word, gazing into each other's eyes.

We began disrobing each other, honorably, with dishonorable intentions. Our peaked caps came off first. I shook out my long, blonde hair, and then shot my fingers into Gordon's curls and gave them a fluff. His smile quivered, like mine. He unbuttoned my tunic, expertly working the buttons with his fingers. The man was deft and skilled, both inside the operating room and out. I popped the buttons on his tunic, also, and at the same time we flung each other's army-issue tops wide open.

Gordon stared at my breasts. I stared at his broad, hairy chest. The sun and my fiancée's eyes felt so wonderful on my cupped breasts. But they, and I, yearned to be totally liberated. Gordon reached around and popped my bra open at the back, as I reached in and ran my hands over his rugged chest.

I shrugged my tunic off and then the hanging bra straps. My breasts surged into the open, my upper body bare. Gordon stripped off his shirt, leaving the both of us bare-chested. Birds chirped in the trees and a gentle breeze blew over us.

We flung our arms around one another, our mouths mashing passionately together. I squeezed Gordon tight to me and he crushed my shimmering body to his, my breasts squishing hotly against his hard chest. Our mouths moved urgently together, our fingernails biting into one another, our hearts thumping as one. At last, we could truly make love, not war.

A burst of Chinese exclamations broke our embrace.

I clutched my arms to my breasts. Gordon grabbed for the Colt .45 revolver on his hip. We held our breath, staring at the bushes where the sound had come from, positioned now to fight or flight as the situation dictated. The war was back and we were caught in the crosshairs, exposed like never before.

Ears pricked and eyes darting, we moved closer to the wall of heavy brush that screened one side of our intimate clearing. There was another gust of Chinese, and then the unmistakable universal sound of grunting and groaning. What the heck was going on behind those bushes?

Gordon held up a hand for me to stay back, and then he advanced further. He cautiously parted some thickly-leaved branches, peered through the bush. My heart was thudding to an old familiar beat now—fear. My arms quivered across my suddenly cold breasts, my hands trembling, breath caught in my throat. As I watched my fiancée stealthily reconnaissance the enemy activity on the other side of that brush, his pistol up and cocked.

Gordon leaned in, looked. Then he lowered his pistol and turned back to me and waved, a smile on his handsome face. I rushed forward to be with him again, utterly relieved, forgetting for the time being that I was utterly naked from the waist up.

I crowded in next to Gordon by the bush and looked through the branches. There was another clearing on the other side. A rough brown blanket was spread out on the green grass, a man and woman on top of the blanket, the both of them naked. Their green woolen People's Volunteer Army uniforms were draped on the branches of a tree on the other side of the clearing. Their entwined nude bodies gleamed in the bright sunshine that flooded the soft spot where *they'd* decided to celebrate the end of hostilities as we had.

I giggled and glanced at Gordon. His grin was ear-to-ear. He aimed his gun at his holster and missed, and the heavy pistol crashed through some branches and thudded to the ground. The loving couple on the blanket instantly ceased their amorous activities and jerked their heads our way.

Gordon sheepishly looked at me and shrugged. I looked at the abandoned uniforms and noted the medical insignias on them, also noted the fact there were no weapons in sight on the other side. So, I took my fiancée's hand and led him around the bushes, through an opening, out into the clearing with the other couple.

They scrambled up onto their elbows, staring at us. They were close to our ages, I could see, smaller than us but both very appealing. The woman had long, dark hair and an oval-shaped face, brown eyes, an upturned nose and full lips, a lean, shapely body with small, taut breasts and a thick bush of black fur between her legs. The man had short dark hair and a slightly square-shaped face, a muscular body, a hard cock that jutted out from a nest of black pubic hairs.

I showed them my breasts in a gesture of goodwill, lifting my arms and the corners of my mouth in friendly greeting. I popped my green pants open and pushed them and my white cotton panties down, stepped out of the dull, conformist uniform totally naked (except for my black boots), into the blazing light of the new day. I was compelled by the giddy excitement brought on by the armistice and the prospect of returning to the States, and the heady excitement of discovering these two beautiful creatures making love in the woods, just as Gordon and I had been about to do. We were at peace, we had so much in common now; we just had to consummate the end of the long war with a gesture that would give pleasure to both sides, to clearly illustrate the total cessation of hostilities.

That was my dizzied thinking, anyway, as I walked hand-in-hand with Gordon up to the lovely couple and sat down on the blanket with them, pulling my fiancée down to their level, as well. I boldly reached out and took the other man's cock in my hand and stroked it. It wasn't an olive branch, but it was just as hard and almost the same color; and even more of a symbol of the end of hate and the beginning of understanding. The man grunted and grinned, his cock surging with heat and strength in my pumping hand.

"What are you doing, Lydia!?" Gordon rasped.

I looked at him, caressing our former enemy's erection. "We're all going to be home soon, Gordon. And we're going to be married—together forever, exclusively. Why not a going-away present, an uplifting end to the war and our singlehood?"

His eyes held doubt. Until the woman reached up and ran her slender fingers through the hair on his chest, smiling seductively at my fiancée. If only women were in charge, I thought at that moment, this war would've ended a whole lot earlier; if it ever would've started.

Gordon looked at the woman, feeling her supple fingers caress his chest, softly tweak his pink nipples. Then he looked at me stroking the man's cock, and a smile brightened his face again. He'd bought into the peace plan, all of us parties to it now.

We haltingly exchanged names—Lydia and Gordon, Chen and Li—and then we excitedly exchanged so much more.

I bent down in between Chen's legs and took the crown of his cock into my mouth and sucked on the swollen head. He groaned and lay back on his elbows, thrusting more of his cock into my mouth. I dipped my head lower and mouthed most of the rigid appendage, bobbing my head up and down, sucking tight and quick on the man's penis. Out of the corner of my eye, I caught Gordon going down on Li next to us on the blanket.

He lay flat on his stomach with his hands gripping Li's spread thighs, bobbing his head in between her legs, lapping the woman's pussy. She squeezed up her breasts, rolled her dark nipples between her fingers, undulating her mound up into my fiancée's face.

Chen put a hand on my head, reminding me of what I was doing, helping me along. I sucked his cock, shooting out my tongue at the base to lick at his balls. His fingers clutched my hair and he thrust more urgently into my suctioning mouth, until I tasted salty pre-cum. I had to remember that the pair had a head start on Gordon and me.

I popped Chen's cock out of my mouth and grasped the slickened appendage and pumped it, watching Gordon lick Li's pussy up and down. My man was good with the human body, especially the female form, both professionally and personally. I tapped him on the shoulder and pointed at Li.

Gordon glanced up at the woman, his lips and chin glistening. He saw that she was quivering on the edge of orgasm, biting her lip with her eyes closed, her hands convulsively clenching her breasts.

He looked at me questioningly. I smiled and showed him the way again, climbing over Chen's waist, then sticking the hood of his cock into my pussy. I sat down on the man's groin, moaning with pleasure as I felt his penis glide up inside of me. He was happy about it, too, reaching up and clasping my hanging breasts, squeezing them.

Gordon didn't need any further demonstration. He jumped to his feet and stripped away his olive drab pants, shedding the last piece of uniform that identified us and them as former enemies. Now, we were all the same, lovers in the flesh, free to play together when once we'd fought.

Gordon's cock jutted out from his ginger loins. He dropped back down to his knees, in between Li's legs again. She wrapped them around his waist and he slotted his big cock into her pussy, falling down on top of her and burying himself inside of Li like Chen was buried inside of me. Talk about rapprochement!

I flattened my palms on Chen's muscle-mounded chest and leaned forward so that he could suck on my swaying breasts, as I undulated on his cock. He filled his mouth with one of my nipples, eagerly tugged on it with his lips, then bounced his head over to my other breast and inhaled and sucked on that buzzingly stiff nipple; as he pumped his cock to and fro in my pussy.

My breasts burned with delicious good feeling, my body bathed in it, my pussy brimming with the hard cock churning inside. I threw back my head and moaned with joy, riding Chen, letting him feed on my breasts and watching my fiancée fuck Chen's woman.

Gordon and Li were wrapped together as Chen and she had been when we'd stumbled onto the pair. Li clung to Gordon's waist with her legs and his neck with her arms, spurring her heels into his humping buttocks. Gordon hugged her, kissed her, slammed his cock back and forth in her pussy, rocking the both of them with their passion, and the both of us. I bounced up and down on Chen's cock, the man grasping my breasts in his hot little hands and pumping up into my pussy in perfect rhythm. The four of us concluded the war with the best kind of bang.

Our moaning and groaning filled the hot air, the crack of damp, heated flesh against damp, heated flesh resounding loud and clear in the electrified atmosphere; no more small arms or heavy gun fire. Gordon and Li swarmed their tongues together, Gordon clasping the woman's shuddering little breasts as he drove into her pussy. I dropped down onto Chen and we wrapped each other up tight, flinging our tongues together in our own erotic dance, his cock pounding into my pussy.

I heard Li and Gordon cry out, and I screamed and Chen grunted. Orgasmic bliss swept through my body, up from Chen's spasming cock in my pussy. I felt his body jerking beneath, his penis spurting inside of me, as I was buffeted by ecstasy.

We'd all surrendered to lust, the aching need to be loved.

As we donned our uniforms afterwards, and then exchanged final kisses and walked away from the scene of carnality, I only wished that we all could've learned this lesson a whole lot earlier.

A LITTLE NIGHT MAGIC
Aiden McKenna

It was on nights like this, when the moonlight fell slick over their bodies through the slats in the blinds, when the cicadas reached a fever pitch and the whole night bucked and thralled with the heat of summer. Nights of naked sweat, of jilting the sheets and sticking to the hardwood floor of the bedroom, knees wet, mouth dry. Thirsty nights. Nights full of heat lightning, when they'd dispense with the pretense of a bed, of silk sheets and down pillows; and they'd fuck, raw as the stars in the cloudless sky. When she'd shed her velvet skin for him, and all bones, they'd dance.

It was a slow dance, all body, no choreography in the slow press of his broad hand against her lower back. Like ships struggling against their mooring as the tide rose within them, helpless to the moon's suggestive pull at the zipper of her dress, the waistband of his jeans. The old, familiar starlight sparking in the pit of their stomachs as their eyes caught. A dry land, all kindling, no rain. Wildfire season. Begging a monsoon. The consumptive, slow dance of bodies on fire, spreading over every inch of bare skin they could reach, the burn of her nails across his back, his entrance into her parted thighs, the tug and pull and consummation. The being consumed.

She loved nights like this, stroking him to a fever pitch and then taking the fullness of him inside her, guiding him home with an artful hand positioned between her thighs, the other hand pinning him to the ground. How she'd rise and fall above him, his sun and moon, this pagan ritual of sweat and slickness nearly cyclical in nature. More spirit than mortal seeking mortal delights, finding her satisfaction in the steady beat of his heart within his chest, a rhythm she'd match with her hips. Nights like this where she'd have him again and again, filling and spilling over, until her thighs trembled and she collapsed on top of him, sated and human once more.

Or nights when he held the curve of her hip and drank her in like a strange fairy wine, intoxicated and enchanted by the earthy taste of her cunt against his lips. He searched like a lost traveler for the places within her that, when touched, would unfurl like a sunflower, leaving her breathless and warm, her toes curling and her back arching with each press of a seeking finger or lap of his tongue. She moved like spring when he touched her that way, swore that she felt morning glories blooming up her spine, making a garden out of her body. When he touched her that way, she came like summer in full bloom.

Before the sun spread across the sky they'd recede, lying tangled like seaweed in a mess of loving bodies and hot breath, pressing slow kisses across shoulder blades and down spines. They reveled in their stickiness, their nakedness, her thighs lying open, his lips mouthing open kisses against her breast. His hand stroking along her inner thigh, testing for leftover currents of electricity. When the new day chased away the night's magic and only they remained, he'd take in the sight of her new as the dawn. Naked and bare in the pale light, she'd open easy for him once more, all wonder and no mystery below him. Just blue light and two bodies, welcoming the morning.

SAGA OF THE SAILMAKER'S WIDOW

Michael Bracken

The sailmaker's widow stood in the doorway of the longhouse that served as both home and shop, watching as a battle-scarred *drekar*—dragon-headed longship—docked and fifty men good and strong swarmed from it, including a broad-shouldered giant wearing a crimson overtunic who stood a head taller than the others. His tightly braided, sun-bleached blond hair hung halfway down his back and his chest-long beard had been braided to match. As she watched, the giant directed the actions of the men unloading the drekar.

"Sigvin?"

She turned at the sound of her name to find Aldreda, a raven-haired thrall her father had brought home from Northumbria following a successful raid when Sigvin was but a child and had included in her dowry when Sigvin married Asbjorn.

"There's a problem with one of the looms."

Sigvin tore her attention from the flurry of activity at the dock and stepped into the longhouse to find one of her thralls staring at a warp-weighted loom. The problem was easy enough to solve, but the young thrall was new to Sigvin and newer still to weaving. Sigvin showed the girl what she had done wrong and put her back to work.

The other thralls were busy at their assigned tasks inside and outside the longhouse, from turning raw wool purchased from Olafr into roving, to spinning roving into yarn, to weaving the yarn into long strips of *vaðmál* that Aldreda would later stitch together with rolled seams and leech ropes before *smörring* the result to finish each sail.

Sigvin's attention returned to the work at hand and she thought no more of the blond giant until a few days later when he filled the doorway of her longhouse. The sight of him so near caused her breath to catch. Her nipples tightened and she felt a long-forgotten tingle of desire at the juncture of her thighs. Ignoring her pounding heart, Sigvin rose to greet him.

He said, "This is Asbjorn's shop?"

"My husband has gone to Valhalla," Sigvin replied. "This is now my shop."

"A warrior, then," said the giant, "and yet he wove sails."

"Do you dishonor my husband's memory with your doubt?"

The blond giant straightened. "I meant no disrespect. I meant only to understand."

Weaving had been women's work for as long as anyone could remember, and that Asbjorn had been known as a sailmaker, despite never having woven a single thread, was testament to both his salesmanship and his confidence in his own manhood. When shipbuilding became more centralized and less the work of individual families, Sigvin's husband had been the first to recognize the need for improved sailmaking productivity. He had built their first looms, acquired their first thralls, and convinced the town's shipbuilders to purchase the first sails they produced. Over time, their trade grew, and when Asbjorn was called to Valhalla, the business became Sigvin's. She explained this to the blond giant.

"Your husband was more than a warrior, then," the blond giant said. "He was a man with vision as well."

"Yes," Sigvin said. "My husband was that."

"I, too, am a man with vision," he said. "May I sit?"

"As you wish."

He removed his sword, placed it on the table between them as they sat, and she could see +VLFBERH+T inlaid on the flat of the blade near the hilt. As they faced one another, the blond giant described the drekar he had commissioned the day before—a ship longer than any before built, with thirty rooms—places for thirty pairs of oars and sixty rowers to man them. "My ship will need a special sail and all agree that Asbjorn—" He paused and corrected himself with a nod to his hostess. "—that Asbjorn's widow is the only sailmaker for the job."

Sigvin nodded to accept his correction.

They discussed the sail's specifications and spent the better part of the afternoon and evening bargaining over a price both found fair. Though outside Sigvin remained focused on their negotiations, inside she found herself a molten pool of desire. They drank horns of ale to seal the deal and only then did she learn the blond giant's name.

"Lars," he said.

"Lars?" she repeated. Only one vikingr named Lars was known to wear a crimson overtunic and carry an Ulfberht sword. "Lars the Invincible?"

The blond giant laughed, the booming sound startling several of the thralls bent over their looms. "Some have called me that."

"Shall I?"

Lars reached across the table and placed his hand over Sigvin's. Her heart skipped a beat as he asked, "Do you fear me?"

The sailmaker's widow stared deep into his pale blue eyes, saw the softness there, and said, "No, I do not."

"Good," he said. "Invincible is a title given me by fearful men."

He released his hold on her hand, stood, and gathered his sword to his side. Sigvin scrambled to her feet, followed Lars out the door and stood watching as he strode away.

Aldreda, who had overheard all that the two had said, stepped up beside her. Before she could speak, Sigvin said, "There's a river of desire between my thighs. I am so wet, I thought I might slide from my seat. I have not felt this way since Asbjorn's passing."

Though Aldreda shared her bed, she did not share the widow's heart. Every day Sigvin missed Asbjorn's laugh, his kiss, and his touch, but never more so than when she prepared for sleep, knowing that he would never again join her.

"Love is like lightning," Aldreda said. "It strikes many places, but only occasionally strikes the same place twice."

Sigvin turned to look at her thrall, surprised that a woman who had never known a man could have such insight. Before she could respond, Aldreda gave her bad news.

"We do not have enough yarn to weave a sail so large as he desires."

"Olafr will soon return." Though Aldreda smiled at Sigvin's mention of the wool merchant, Sigvin had less pleasant thoughts as she continued. "Let us pray that his trip has been a success."

"Yes," Aldreda said. She hid her smile behind her hand and turned away.

Sigvin spent the rest of her day with her thoughts torn asunder. Though she tried to concentrate on the tasks at hand—which included finishing a sail due before the next washing day and finishing another due before the next full moon—her thoughts repeatedly returned to Lars the Invincible. For the first time since Asbjorn's death, she found herself imagining what it might be like to be with another man, to feel his weight upon her and to feel his pleasure giver within her. She felt warmth spread through her body each time she imagined lying with Lars and her thoughts were confused. Did she dishonor her dead husband with her thoughts and with her feelings?

That night, as they prepared for bed, Sigvin revealed her confusion to Aldreda, who asked, "But what of Olafr the wool merchant?"

Sigvin often suspected Olafr was more interested in her business than her body or her brain. "Despite his repeated entreaties, I have no interest in Olafr. He is too old—"

Ten winters older than Sigvin, Aldreda said, "He is my age!"

"—and too round."

"But he is handsome and successful," protested Aldreda, "as successful a wool merchant as Asbjorn was a sailmaker."

Startled by her thrall's impudence, Sigvin stared at the older woman for a moment before recognizing in Aldreda's comments about Olafr a mirror of the feelings she had for the blond giant. "You have feelings for Olafr?"

"I…" Aldreda cast her eyes down.

Sigvin laughed and enveloped Aldreda in a hug. "The ways of the heart are never so obvious as when we wear them upon our sleeve."

Two evenings later, after the sun slipped below the horizon on washing day, when only the light from the central fire illuminated the longhouse and everyone within was preparing for slumber, Lars again appeared in the doorway. Sigvin invited him in with a question. "What cause for your return?"

Lars took Sigvin's arm and pulled her close. As he stared down into her eyes, he said, "I cannot stop thinking about you."

"Nor I you," Sigvin admitted.

He covered her mouth with his, the fullness of his beard engulfing her face, and he kissed her. She parted her lips, his tongue found the opening, and soon their tongues wrestled.

She wanted the blond giant as much as he wanted her and they began to strip away one another's clothing as she pulled him toward the rear of the longhouse where she kept her bed.

Sigvin shared living quarters with her thralls, so they would have no privacy and expected none. Aldreda saw their approach and scrambled out of the bed she shared with Sigvin before the two lovers could reach her, finding refuge on the far side of the longhouse. Sigvin's nakedness was not unknown to her and she knew that even though Sigvin had the soft curves of a woman, they masked the strength of a man.

Sigvin had only ever been with one man, so she knew not what to expect. As the blond giant's clothes fell away, she found his thickly muscled body free of blemish, for he had never felt the prick of another man's blade nor felt the crushing blow of another man's axe, and his erect pleasure giver was unlike her dead husband's, more a mighty oaken mast than a blunt-headed bludgeon.

Lars pushed Sigvin down on her bed, took her ankles in his hands and spread her legs wide. Then he knelt between them and buried his face between her thighs. His beard tickled, but she did not laugh. Instead, she grabbed fistfuls of his hair and pulled his face tight against her female opening. He licked her swollen lips and traced the entire length of her slit as the womanly scent of her filled his nostrils and her desire moistened his facial hair.

Sigvin spread her legs wider still and Lars thrust his tongue inside her, drew it back, and plunged it in a second time. Then he found her swollen pleasure button and he stroked it with his tongue until her hips began bucking up and down, her pubic bone bouncing against his nose. As he tongued her faster and faster, she pulled his face tighter against her female opening.

So much time had passed since she had last felt this escalation of sexual tension that she was not quite prepared. Her thighs quivered around the blond giant's ears, and then she came with a familiar gasp she had not experienced since her final coupling with Asbjorn.

Aldreda, having escaped from her usual sleeping arrangement just in time to keep from being pushed aside, sat on the opposite side of the longhouse, her back against the wall and her knees drawn up. She had watched Sigvin with Asbjorn before he was called to Valhalla, but nothing they had ever done compared to the expression of lust she watched unfolding before her.

Lars slid upward, preparing to mount the widow, but she stopped him. He was too big, too heavy, and she feared being crushed. She rolled him onto his back. His erect pleasure giver rose upward from the tangled nest of his blond pubic hair. From across the room, Aldreda marveled at the size of it until Sigvin straddled Lars.

She adjusted her position until the swollen head of his pleasure giver pressed against the wet folds of her female opening. Then she dropped her entire weight into his lap, impaling herself on his mighty mast. She pressed her hands on Lars's chest and rode him as if in a drekar riding the waves in a storm-tossed sea. Her breasts bounced wildly up and down and Lars grabbed them, capturing each one in his massive hands. Her turgid nipples strained against his palms and he began thrusting his hips upward to meet each of Sigvin's downward thrusts.

As Sigvin rode the blond giant's mighty mast, Aldreda slipped one hand beneath her clothing and touched herself in a way that brought the pleasure she wished Olafr would someday bring her.

Sigvin and Lars fucked hard and fucked fast, the bed beneath them threatening to break with each of Sigvin's downward thrusts. On the far side of the room, Aldreda came first and she bit her bottom lip to keep from crying out and attracting attention to herself.

Then Sigvin came just as Lars thrust into her one final time and fired a thick rope of manly effluent deep into her throbbing female opening. She collapsed on top of the blond giant, flattening her breasts against his chest, and she lay with her face buried in his beard as her female opening clenched and unclenched around his shrinking oaken mast.

Lars returned each night for the next several nights and, though their lovemaking was not nearly as violently energetic, it made Sigvin forget about the other man in her life. So, she was surprised when Olafr returned from his wool-buying trip. She was standing outside her longhouse near the end of the day, directing one of the thralls in the dying of a skein of wool, when Olafr approached. She greeted him politely but without the warmth he desired. "Was your trip a success? I have need for much wool."

Olafr answered her question with an accusation. "You have entertained another man."

"So what if I have?"

"I have made my intentions clear," Olafr said, "and in this way you insult me."

"I have no desire for you," Sigvin told the wool merchant, "and I have made that clear at every opportunity."

Lars the Invincible approached from behind the wool merchant, arriving for his nightly tryst with the sailmaker's widow. His arrival interrupted their conversation.

When Olafr realized who had joined them, he demanded, "Is this the man?"

Sigvin could not and did not deny it.

Olafr spun on the blond giant. "The sight of you offends me."

Lars stopped. He glanced at Sigvin and then back at the wool merchant.

"I am at a disadvantage," Lars said, "for we have not been introduced."

"You have lain with my woman."

"I am not your woman!" Sigvin insisted through gritted teeth.

Olafr ignored her protestations and drew his battleaxe.

Aldreda had just stepped out of the longhouse with two strips of *vaðmál* meant for a byrding ship's sail as Lars the Invincible drew his sword. Neither man carried a shield and both Aldreda and Sigvin knew the wool merchant had provoked a fight he could not win.

"No!" Aldreda shouted as she ran toward the two men, her arms filled with the *vaðmál* she'd been preparing to stitch together. As the two men approached one another, she threw the sailcloth onto them, surprising the two antagonists.

As Lars and Olafr struggled to untangle their weapons from the sailcloth, Sigvin stepped between the two would-be combatants. "This must stop."

The blond giant sheathed his sword. "I did not know you were spoken for," he said, proving that in matters of the heart he could, perhaps, be scarred.

"But I am not," Sigvin protested.

"No matter what I feel in my heart," Lars the Invincible said. "I should not have lain with you."

"But…"

Lars stared at Sigvin and she knew her protestations fell on deaf ears. A man for whom she did not care had claimed her and nothing she could say to the blond giant would change that.

As Lars walked away, she turned on the wool merchant. "You presumptuous swine. I don't want you. I've never wanted you. I've only been accommodating your attentions because I need your wool."

"And which I may never again provide!" Olafr turned and stalked off.

"All is lost," Sigvin told Aldreda after the two men had gone and they were examining the sailcloth, fearful it might have been damaged by the thrall's impetuous actions several heartbeats earlier.

"What have I done?" Sigvin asked. "I had two men and now I have none."

Aldreda stared at Sigvin and spoke as she had never spoken before. "You are but a foolish girl. You have loved and been loved and had the attentions of men, while I have only loved from afar, watching as the man I desire plied you with his attention."

Sigvin looked up into her eyes. "Olafr?"

Aldreda nodded. "Is it not possible for lightning to strike each and every one of us?"

The next several days only brought additional grief to the sailmaker's widow. She finished and delivered two sails but lacked the wool to begin work on the sail commissioned by Lars the Invincible. Repeated entreaties to Olafr were as beneficial as spitting into the wind and Sigvin's thralls grew idle.

While lying in bed one evening several days after Aldreda had prevented Olafr's certain death, the two women discussed possible resolutions. Finally, Aldreda could hold back no longer, and she said, "If I were a freewoman, I could tell Olafr of my love."

Sigvin stared at the thrall her family had owned since her own childhood. "And if Olafr would relinquish his claim to my affections, I would be free to declare mine for Lars."

The two women stared at one another in the dim light and then Sigvin captured Aldreda's face between her hands. She kissed her thrall full on the lips and, when the kiss ended, said, "It is done."

Only it wasn't. The gift of freedom was the occasion for a feast the next washing day, during which Aldreda fastened her slave collar to a sheep and then severed the sheep's head. She removed the bloody slave collar and presented the collar to Sigvin, her former master, as a symbol of her newfound freedom. What followed was a feast in which the food was plentiful, the ale flowed freely, and nearly everyone in town but Lars and his crew partook.

Sigvin saw to it that her thralls kept Olafr plied with drink throughout the feast, and midway between sunset and sunrise, the wool merchant stumbled back to his longhouse, Aldreda only a few steps behind.

The next morning Aldreda returned to Sigvin's longhouse wearing a smile as broad as a fjord. She told her former master, "You shall have your wool."

"What have you done?" Sigvin asked.

"When Olafr woke and found me naked in his bed, he demanded to know how I had come to be there. I told him he had invited me and that he had been quite proficient with his pleasure maker."

"And was he?"

"Stone drunk," Aldreda said. "He could not have raised his mast with the help of an entire ship's crew."

The two women laughed.

"But he need never know that," Aldreda continued. "I told Olafr how many years I had ached for his attention and his touch—which is no lie—and now that I'd had it—which is!—I would gladly profess my love to all who listened. Olafr is no fool. To have the love of one woman good and pure means more to him than to spend eternity pining after a woman he knows in his heart he can never have."

Sigvin pulled Aldreda into her arms and the two women hugged.

That afternoon Olafr delivered all the wool Sigvin needed for Lars the Invincible's sail and enough more that she could begin work on a smaller sail as well. That evening, after she had all of her thralls busy once again, Sigvin went in search of Lars.

She found him sitting at the table in the longhouse he had called home during the time he had been in town, and she stood in the doorway until Lars stood and motioned her inside. She stopped when they stood a mere hand width apart and said, "I come to you free of commitment, without obligation to another."

"Olafr visited me earlier today," Lars said. "He told me he has forfeited his claim on you."

"But he never had me!"

"You protest too much," Lars said as he pulled the sailmaker's widow into his arms and covered her mouth with his to silence her.

The silencing kiss quickly grew passionate. He cleared the table with a sweep of his arm and then he spun her around. He bent her over the table, flipped her dress over her back and drew down her underthings.

Though she could not see what he was doing, Sigvin knew he had pushed aside his own clothing to press the head of his erect pleasure giver against her female opening. She was already wet with desire and he drove into her with little resistance, drew back and drove into her again.

Sigvin held tight to the table as Lars grabbed her hips and fucked her with an ever-increasing rhythm, his mighty oaken mast driving deep inside her, his pleasure giver sliding in and out of her. He reached around and under her clothing until he could press the tip of one thick finger against the cleft of her female opening and stroke her pleasure button in counter-rhythm to the strokes of his pleasure giver.

Sigvin came and then Lars came, filling her with a thick rope of his manly effluent. She barely had time to catch her breath before he stepped back, lifted her off her feet, and carried her to his bed. Soon their clothes were strewn about them and this time he made slow, deliberate love to the sailmaker's widow.

That night, at much the same time that Sigvin and Lars coupled, Aldreda learned of Olafr's prowess with his pleasure giver and she was pleased. The next morning she told Sigvin, "Olafr was every bit the master lover I had dreamed him to be."

That day Aldreda moved her things from Sigvin's longhouse to Olafr's, yet she remained in Sigvin's employ until she taught Sigvin's other thralls how to stitch together two strips of *vaðmál* with rolled seams and how to properly affix leech ropes.

Lars moved his things to Sigvin's longhouse and shared her bed and her heart through the winter. The following spring, Sigvin stood on the dock and watched as Lars the Invincible's new drekar, complete with the sail she and her thralls had made, sailed out of the harbor on its way to raid Northumbria.

No longer the sailmaker's widow, but now the Invincible's wife, Sigvin's heart burst with the joy she thought lost upon Asbjorn's death, and she knew she would watch the harbor every day until the rising tide brought her new lover's return.

ABOUT THE AUTHORS

Although he is the author of several books, including the private eye novel *All White Girls*, two-time Derringer Award-winning writer **Michael Bracken** is better known as the author of more than 1,100 short stories. His erotica has appeared in or is forthcoming in *Best Gay Romance 2015*, *Fifty Shades of Green*, *Fifty Shades of Grey Fedora*, *Flesh & Blood: Guilty as Sin*, *Hot Blood: Strange Bedfellows*, *Sex Objects*, *The Mammoth Book of Best New Erotica 4*, and in many other anthologies and periodicals. He lives and writes in Texas.

Morrigan Cox has always felt at home in the natural beauty of Arizona, where she discovered an affinity for heat that goes beyond the oven-like temperature of the desert. With an appreciation for beauty in all things, she explores story ideas from different perspectives and follows her curiosity into creativity. The best time of the day to find her writing is during the long afternoons when the sun is baking the ground around the saguaros standing sentinel in the yard. Tucked away inside with her cattle dog, Gila, Morrigan will be typing away, waiting for the stars to pin the night sky with their brilliance. Always a voracious reader, Morrigan has enjoyed giving voice to the stories in her head, and is eager to share them with others.

When **Paul Henry** taught creative writing and composition in the public schools, he posted his rejection slips on the classroom bulletin board. Now, he teaches communications studies and performance at a small Midwestern college. Paul believes that writers should follow Martin Luther's advice to "sin boldly." Among his fictional heroes are an angel who stops by Gomorrah, a psychic real estate agent, and the twin brother of Jesus. He has published over eighty short stories, plus the novella *Bridge Games*. Two of his stories have been nominated for the Pushcart Prize. *Fringe Magazine* called his story, *Chicken's Revenge*, "the most insane thing you are ever likely to read." Paul's wife and best critic, Pamela, admits that his fiction sometimes frightens her. His latest novel, *Twenty-one Humiliating Demands* chronicles an aging assassin who takes a sabbatical to teach Atrocity Studies.

Rachael Knight is an Australian writer of erotica and science fiction, and especially loves combining the two. She recently graduated from university with a literature degree and after three years of learning how to write "serious fiction," she realized that writing about sex was way more fun. Rachael is currently working on a post-apocalyptic romance novel, which she hopes will be as much fun to read as it is to write!

Lynn Lake's writing credits include many erotic magazines and websites, stories in the anthologies *Chocolate Flava 3* & *4*, *Readerotica 2, 3, 4* & *7*, *The Mammoth Book of Lesbian Erotica*, and *The Mammoth Book of Erotic Confessions*, and the standalone novella *The Red Scare*.

Artist and writer **Parker Lee** lives and works in a small town, where the good southern soil is made of slick red clay—a potter's delight and a gardener's nightmare. We love amending things here: dirt, history, unrequited loves, and if you liked Parker Lee's little vignette, *Venus Flirting with Jupiter on the Backside of the Crescent Moon*, by all means check out her e-book, *Erotica: Sexy Little Stories for Friends & Lovers*.

Aiden McKenna is a writer and editor living out her dream in the dirty south with her beautiful wife and her unruly pet ferret. A bad Catholic and a good Christian, she considers herself one part June Cleaver and one part meat cleaver. Her undergraduate degree is in theatre, but most of the important moments of her life happen backstage at punk shows. When not on tour or tied up by writing deadlines, she enjoys time spent with family on her farm and relaxing on the front porch in the southern heat, with a strong drink and a scintillating novel. She believes in the power of shower sex, in scissoring, and in eating dessert in bed. More than that, she believes in the power of the potential energy contained inside a pen to change the world. McKenna has previously published erotica with Torquere Press.

Chase Morgan is your average guy with a mind that tends to drift while out to dinner with friends or during work meetings. His wayward thoughts vacillate between naughty things that could be done in public to pondering whether the Sasquatch jerks off in the woods. Mr. Morgan's friends are far from boring; he's just really good at multi-tasking. He began writing erotica for his wife while away on business trips. As his muse and biggest supporter, she encouraged him to take a stab at sharing his unruly mind with the world. She doesn't wonder about Sasquatch's masturbatory habits, but she is great at humoring him when his mind takes off in the woods. His current works can be found in *The Sexy Librarian's Big Book of Erotica*, *The Dirty Thirty*, *Desire Behind Bars*, and a couple episodes on Rose Caraway's *The Kiss Me Quick* podcast.

Leah Mueller is a writer who resides in western Washington. Her work has been published in *Cultured Vultures*, *Origins Journal, Quail Bell*, *Typoetic, Talking Soup*, Silver Birch Press, *Semaphore, MaDCap*, *The Rain, Party*, and *Disaster Society*, and many others. Leah's chapbook, *Queen of Dorksville* was published in 2012 by Crisis Chronicles Press. Leah's new book of poetry and prose, entitled *Allergic to Everything* was recently published by Writing Knights Press. Her book of erotic short stories, *The Underside of the Snake* will be published by Red Ferret Press in January 2016. Leah was a featured reader and poet in July 2015 at the New York Poetry Festival, and also at the Death Rattle Poetry Festival in Idaho in October, 2015. She enjoys sunflowers, lucid dreaming, sensual pleasures, and anything water-related.

Sophia Soror spends most of her time between the covers with her Muse or bent over her writing desk. She is fascinated by the alchemy of transmuting the prima materia of inspiration into ink and constructing entire worlds with the written word. In a deep cavern somewhere, at the end of a labyrinth of tunnels, she keeps her secret workshop. There she sweats away until her skin is smudged black with pigments as she etches stories into her Muse's skin. In the parts of her life not consumed by erotica, Sophia is an award-winning playwright, a teacher, and a doctoral candidate in mythology.

Autmn Tooley lives in Seattle, WA. She has a whimsical love of fairies and folk tales from around the world. When she isn't crunching numbers by day, she can often be found enjoying one of the many geek-themed coffees at Wayward Coffeehouse and writing. This is her first published work.

Alegra Verde, originally a public relations professional and aspiring poet, began her second life as a writer of erotic fiction in 2009. That same year, Virgin Black Lace published two of her stories. Since then, her fiction has appeared in anthologies published by Avon, Zane, Cleis, Logical Lust and others. Harlequin's Mira Spice published two novellas from her *Glory* series as e-books and later translated them into several different languages for print anthologies. In 2015, Boroughs published two of her novellas, *Lights Off, Lights On* and *The Commitment*. A Japanese translation of her Regency short, *The Engagement Party*, which originally appeared in Avon's *Lords, Ladies, Butlers & Maids*, will be released in early 2016. On her free website, she posts short stories and a serialized paranormal novel entitled *The Revelers*. Verde, who holds a doctorate in English Literature, lives in Detroit where she teaches writing and literature at a local college. When class ends, like Diana Prince, she takes off her glasses and ventures forth amassing fodder for her fiction because there is always "a new journey to be started, a new promise to be fulfilled, a new page to be written" (Wonder Woman #62).

Cherry Wild is new to writing erotica seriously, though the sex scenes in her novels have been spiraling out of polite control for some time now, and she has been reading erotica for decades. She is working on far too many projects, but financing beach vacations and cabana boys is very motivating. Under her legal name, Cherry is an internationally read technical writer (which can be raunchier than you might imagine), working on a murder mystery series, and is a published poet. She was the Managing Editor of her university's undergraduate literary magazine for two years and Cherry spent over five years working closely with the publishing industry for a famous high-tech company. A redhead, Cherry can confirm that the rumors are true.

www.ingramcontent.com/pod-product-compliance
Lightning Source LLC
Chambersburg PA
CBHW020744130626
46554CB00006B/2137